THE CHARMED CIRCLE

by Dorothea J. Snow

cover and decorations by

Mimi Korach

A WHITMAN BOOK

Western Publishing Company, Inc., Racine, Wisconsin

WHITMAN is a registered trademark of Western Publishing Company, Inc.

Library of Congress Catalog Card Number: 62-15253

CONTENTS

1

Don't Panic

Shoulders drooping, Lauralee Larkin sat on the edge of one of the twin beds in the room she shared with her older sister, Maxine. In all her fourteen years her spirits had never reached so low an ebb.

"I wish this day had never come!" she moaned softly, hugging to her, as though for comfort, a stuffed, long-legged, violently spotted cloth giraffe. "I hate it!"

With despairing eyes she looked out the window of her comfortable brick English Colonial home in suburban Elm Park and, seeing nothing beyond the swaying branch of the tree outside, she added, "I knew I would!"

For ages, it seemed, she had been sure of it, mostly since that day in July when her best friend, Jenny Moore, had moved with her family to San Francisco. Last week on registration day her feeling had been partially confirmed. And now on the first day of school she was positive of it.

Binky, her tow-headed, ten-year-old brother, stuck his freckled face through the doorway of her room. "Better get down to breakfast pronto," he grinned, showing the two, big, new front teeth that made him look exactly like a certain rabbit character of comic book fame. "Everybody's there but you and me, and I soon will be." He heaved his plaid-shirted shoulders in an exaggerated sigh and added, "Boy, are you lucky!"

Then he turned and loped down the stairs as silently as a stampeding buffalo.

Lauralee stared dully after him. *Lucky,* he had said. Well, she supposed he would, in his childish way, think she should be proud and happy to leave junior high behind and go into the practically grown-up world of high school.

How wrong he was.

It was that very difference that made her dread it so. Give others the new and untried things if they wanted them; she preferred the old and familiar and predictable.

She had been so happy in junior high. She had had Jenny then and they had shared so many wonderful times. She had never wanted that changed. If only Mr. Moore's firm had not transferred him to California. That move had shattered the lives of both the girls.

"Lee! Lauralee!" Mrs. Larkin's voice came, gently chiding, up the stairs and down the hall to her daughters' room overlooking the rear garden. "Breakfast is ready, dear."

Lauralee sniffled. Even Mother hadn't been very understanding.

"You will get over it, pet," she had said, ruffling Lauralee's short brown hair. "As you grow older you will find yourself saying hello and good-bye to people quite often."

But not to such special *people as Jenny,* she had wanted to cry out.

She must be brave though. Jenny had said in her last

letter, which had come yesterday, that she was trying to be. There would be other girls from her junior high class going to Willowlake. She'd make friends with them. And she had always really *liked* school.

Lauralee straightened up determinedly. No matter what, she would not let her feelings show. Patting Goop, her giraffe, as fondly as though he were alive she placed him in the center of her hollowed-out pillow. Inserting what she knew was a falsely cheerful note into her voice, she answered, "Coming, Mother."

Then, just as suddenly, the air went out of her ballooning bravery. She slumped again, sinking back into her pond of despair. There would be other girls at Willowlake that she knew and could make friends with, yes. But would they want to make friends with her? How could she have ever imagined, even for a second, that the coming years in high school could ever be anywhere near as happy as those that had gone before?

Memories of her junior high days came back in waves and all but swept her under. Every morning, she was sure now, she had awakened with a song on her lips, had straightened her room, and been downstairs before breakfast was half ready. She had helped Mother finish preparing the meal, had eaten quickly, rinsed her dishes and put them into the dishwasher. Then she had skipped over to Jenny's house, right across the street, in plenty of time to walk to Elm Park Junior High School with her friend—except when Jenny had been a little quicker and arrived at her house first.

"*Lauralee!*" That was her father's voice and it had a

definite let's-not-have-any-more-of-this-nonsense ring to it. "Come down and eat your breakfast!"

Lauralee jumped as if she had been shot. She snatched up the sheaf of printed material she had gathered on registration day. On top was a booklet entitled *Know Your Willowlake Community High School*. With every page she had read of it she had grown more gloomy.

For Willowlake was, first of all, a huge school with an enrollment of thousands. The buildings, beautiful, modern, and up-to-date in equipment, sprawled over a tree-shaded campus. It looked more like a college than a high school. Compared to the several junior high schools in the township, from which it drew its pupils, it was an awesome place indeed.

"I'll be lost here," Lauralee had thought dismally when, on registration day, she had wandered down one of its long corridors. One needed the map of the buildings that was given out with all the other forms and cards and sheets of instructions. It was an elaborate diagram, showing the location of every room and facility. But looking it over only made Lauralee more confused than ever.

If only Jenny were going to that awful place with her. At least then she wouldn't be alone in her misery.

Hugging her booklet to her, along with fee cards, class schedules, notebook and pencil, she started toward the door. She was glad now that she had left her books in her locker when she had bought them that day after registration. In the state of mind she was in now she would do well just to get herself to school.

Passing the full-length mirror on the closet door she

caught a quick glance at her reflection. It gave her no comfort.

She wasn't ugly, she told herself, but she was no beauty either. Tall for her fourteen years, and slim almost to the point of thinness, she seemed to herself all arms and legs. "And feet," she often added, "like gunboats." Her father often tried to comfort her about this saying it was really a good thing to have a firm foundation.

She could never be fluffily feminine, she knew. With her skin tanned and her brown hair bleached from swimming and sunning to almost the same nutlike shade, she was much too healthy looking for that. Her eyes were her best point, she thought critically, being gray and wide set and heavily fringed with lashes a bit lighter than she wished they were. And she thought her brows, though well-shaped, were too scraggly looking.

"My mouth," she thought wryly, "looks like the Grand Canyon." But her teeth were straight so she hadn't had to wear braces. Jenny had had to wear the horrid things and Lauralee knew well how her friend had hated them.

Until now, though, her looks hadn't weighed heavily upon her. She had had Jenny and Jenny had had her and they would have liked each other if both had looked like witches on Spook Night! But now, she suspected uneasily, it was going to be different in that department, too!

"*Lauralee!*" Her father had reached the limit of his patience.

"Well, don't beat me," she muttered and down the stairs she went. But there was no spring in her step nor lilt in her spirits.

As she sat down listlessly at the dining-room table, her eye caught the flash of the flame-colored mums that bordered the back yard of her home. If only she could feel as perky as they looked. Always before, the turning leaves of autumn, the invigorating tang of the air and the prospect of school had sent shivers of pure delight through her. But then that had been before Jenny had left.

Her father looked up over the top of the sports page of an early morning Chicago paper. His usually twinkling brown eyes impaled her through the horn-rimmed spectacles.

"There is a school bus that stops at a certain nearby corner," he said sternly, "at exactly seven-fifteen. I expect you and Maxine to be out there in time to board it each morning."

Carefully he turned another page and folded it just so. His coffee cup stopped in mid-air when he added, "I will drive you to school *only* in case of emergency."

"Yes, sir," Lauralee answered meekly, unfolding her napkin and arranging it on the lap of her beige pleated skirt.

She knew why her father was making an issue of her getting to the bus on time. He had seen a neighbor friend play chauffeur to a lazy daughter for four years, driving her to school every time she missed the bus, which was as often as she could manage. Mr. Larkin had repeatedly made it clear to her and Maxine that he would not be so put upon.

Not that he had to remind Maxine—not rise-and-shine Maxine, now almost finished with her breakfast. Nobody ever had to tell her when and how to do anything. It seemed as if she did the right things at the right time and in the right way as automatically as the coming of morning.

If only she could be like Maxine, Lauralee thought now, efficient, accomplished, *perfect*. No wonder her older sister, a senior now, was the apple of her parents' eyes.

Small, pert, and pretty, that was Maxine, with pink-and-white complexion that made her look healthy, too, and yet somehow frail and dainty. Also she was smart, and popular. Boys gravitated to her like bees to a clover blossom.

"Lauralee Larkin simply can't hold a candle to her sister, Maxine." Lauralee had long imagined that remark being made by family friends and others who had opportunities to compare them. "They are so different one would never think they were sisters," and so on and on.

Lauralee had always felt that her parents compared her to her sister, too, usually unfavorably.

Now that she and Maxine were going to the same school, it would be worse, with teachers and counselors doing the same. Lauralee shuddered. Could she stand a whole year of that? Next year, of course, Maxine would be going away to college and the sharpness of their difference would fade, she hoped.

Maxine sat across from her now. No worries lurked behind that smooth, serene brow beneath the shining blond hair falling shoulder length in a page-boy bob. With her blue eyes and dimpling smile she could easily model for a picture of the All American Girl—and without make-up, except for a bit of powder on her turned-up nose and a trace of lipstick. It had to be a trace or Dad would notice and make her wipe it off.

"I'll not have my daughters going around looking like

clowns," he often said firmly, "with a lot of goo on their faces."

Lauralee had almost told him once that he had a daughter who looked like a clown even without make-up. But, of course, she knew that wasn't quite true. Still, compared to Maxine, everything about *her* was all wrong.

She wasn't jealous of Maxine, though; she just wished she were more like her. "I'd bleach my hair if I thought I could get away with it," she thought now and looked at her father and knew she couldn't.

"Eat your waffle, dear." Mother's words penetrated the cotton-wool padding of her thoughts, sounding muffled and far away. Nothing seemed real to Lauralee this morning. It was all a dream, a bad dream, this thing of Jenny being gone and she. . . . Why, she'd wake up soon and skip across the street and join her friend and they would go to junior high together.

She had always felt at ease with Jenny. In looks, personality, and brain power they were on the same plane, and she was sure Jenny had never compared her to *anybody*.

Absent-mindedly she put a square of butter on each little section of her waffle. Then she poured maple syrup over the top until the waffle threatened to float out onto the table.

Maxine gasped. "Oh, the calories!" she cried, squeezing her eyes shut as though she could not stand the sight. Then she added in the tone of a martyr, "I ate mine with no butter or syrup at all."

Lauralee grinned smugly. "Each to his own," she said grimly, and began to eat with exaggerated relish. That was one advantage she had over Maxine; she could eat anything she liked and as much as she wanted and never gain an ounce. But her sister, tending to be plumpish like Mother, had to watch every bite to keep the sweet curves that were so attractive now.

"There are some advantages in being built like a bean-pole, I guess, eh, Dad?" Lauralee winked at her father. He winked back. He ate anything he wanted, too, and was always teasing his wife about her dieting.

At that Maxine bounced up from the table, picked up her plate, glass, and silver and disappeared into the kitchen. Splashing water told Lauralee that Maxine was rinsing her dishes and stacking them in the dishwasher. Lauralee sighed silently. She'd gladly trade her eating privilege for the efficiency and other virtues of her sister.

"Bye, everybody!" Maxine put her head back into the dining room. A pink sweater thrown over a brown sheath set off her dainty blondness and made her look like something off a birthday cake.

"Bye, kitten," said her father fondly, and all the others said good-bye, too. The door slammed and Maxine's skipping steps soon faded away. Maxine liked to get to the corner early, she said, so she could talk to a couple of girl friends. Lauralee knew of another reason for her sister's haste, however, and that was Tiny Adams, a husky, six-foot athletic senior who also managed to get there early.

She wished Dad would call her kitten—just once—even though she knew how ludicrous that would sound, for she looked about as kittenish as a full-grown moose.

"You have twenty minutes, dear," her mother reminded

her. Her father rattled his paper as though in emphasis.

Lauralee took another waffle. She wasn't going to go to school hungry or get to that bus stop one second sooner than she had to. Though there would be neighborhood girls there that she knew, there would be no close friend with whom she could exchange confidences. She and Jenny had been all-in-all to each other ever since their days in the fourth grade. Neither had bothered to try to make other close friends. Besides, she'd have little in common with the other girls since she had been visiting her grandmother's cottage at a Wisconsin lake ever since Jenny had left.

Her cloud of loneliness settled about her closer than ever. Her classes, she did not doubt, would be made up mostly of girls she wouldn't even know from other junior high schools. Jenny! How could it happen that we should ever be separated? Her gulp of self-pity was so noisy that her mother frowned in disapproval of her table manners.

Father again peered over the top of his paper, which was now turned to the financial page. "Ten minutes until bus time," he reminded her gruffly.

Sudden tears welled up in Lauralee's eyes. "Stop picking on me!" she wailed, and wondered if that voice crying out as though in pain was really hers.

"Boo hoo!" Binky jeered unfeelingly.

Father's paper crackled as he folded it and laid it beside his plate. He rose quickly. "You take it from here." He grinned as he kissed his wife, muttered good-bye, and left.

"If Mother says one word, I'll *explode*," Lauralee thought defiantly. But Mother kept a serene countenance and put another waffle on Binky's plate.

The roar of the car's motor sounded from the garage. Through the window Lauralee could see the top of the car over a bridal wreath bush. It backed out of the driveway and was gone, headed, she knew, for the rush-hour traffic on North Avenue, that led from Elm Park into Chicago's loop and her father's office on La Salle Street.

Lauralee felt contrite. She shouldn't have said what she had. She had a wonderful father and she knew it. Often she and Mother stopped in at his office when they were downtown shopping. Located on the thirty-sixth floor of the building, it offered a beautiful view. From one corner window she could see far out over Lake Michigan and, from another, she could look down on the Windy City's teeming north side.

Mr. Larkin was comptroller of a company making gasoline station pumps, among other things, and Lauralee supposed he made a lot of money. He kept his family in very comfortable circumstances though he often complained about the big bills that came in every month.

Mother sighed. "Weekday mornings. Rush, rush, rush!"

She poured more batter into the waffle iron. Binky apparently had a bottomless pit for a stomach, and plenty of time to fill it. Classes at Elm Park Grade School started later than those in high school and the building itself was only three blocks from the Larkin house.

Lowering the top of the iron, Mrs. Larkin looked over at Lauralee. "Did you make your bed and hang up your clothes this morning, Lee?" she asked.

"Nope," Binky answered for her. "Her side of the room looks like it had been hit by Hurricane Hannah!"

Lauralee glared at him. There was nothing pestier than a small brother, she was sure. Anyhow, how did Mother expect her to find time to do all that before she left for school? But Maxine had. She remembered Max's bed had been made and her side of the room they shared was as neat as the proverbial pin.

"I'll do it after school," she promised lamely. Where did the time go? Hastily now she picked up her dishes and took them to the kitchen. But a glance at the clock on the wall there told her she didn't have time to rinse and stack them in any dishwasher. So she left them on the counter and started on a run for the hall closet.

"Bye, Mom!" she called back through the hall. "See you this afternoon."

Mother answered but Lauralee didn't hear what she said. Grabbing a sweater from a hanger, she started out the front door and down the steps.

"Oh, bugs!" she cried when, looking down, she saw she had grabbed Mother's old sweater, the one she wore while working with her flowers. Back Lauralee ran and, making sure she had the right one this time, grabbed her own brown one and left.

Head down, jogging along, she saw nothing but the tips of her brown suede flats. Suddenly she looked up, just in time to see the big yellow bus with WILLOWLAKE COMMUNITY HIGH SCHOOL sprawled in black letters along its side. It was pulling away from the bus stop and snorting down Grantley Avenue!

Lauralee stopped in her tracks. She could have cried. Was the whole world arrayed against her? She had known today would not be pleasant, but did it have to be so grim?

How could she get to school on time now? It was a good two miles away and there was no city bus to take her there. Dad was gone and she couldn't have called this an emergency anyway. Mother's small car was in the garage for repairs.

"Oh, me, oh, my!" she moaned, as helpless as a feather in a high wind. Why did she have to live so far from school? An unexcused absence would mean she could not make up any work she might miss. She had read that in the booklet.

Booklet? Where was it? And her cards, and schedules, and. . . .

"Don't panic!" Binky's voice came from behind her. She whirled and saw him, grinning at her. In his hands was the stack of printed matter she had left on the floor beside her chair in the dining room. Cheerfully he handed it to her and walked unconcernedly on toward his own school.

He didn't care how she got to school, that was plain.

Don't panic, indeed.

2

Alone in a Crowd

For several seconds Lauralee stood, unable to move. In dreams she sometimes found herself in this very predicament, feeling desperately that she must hurry somewhere but, in spite of frantic efforts, immobilized, her feet seemingly glued to the ground. Then, at the crucial moment, she had always awakened to find herself in bed, snug between the covers, with no necessity for going anywhere. The sweet relief that would sweep through her then. But now. . . .

"What in the world am I going to do?" she wailed to herself.

She could walk, of course, but she could never get there before the tardy bell rang. Being tardy would only add to her first-day problems.

She was so awash in woe that she did not see or hear the blue sedan approach and slow down at the corner. Not until the warm, friendly voice of a neighbor, Mrs. Newton, drifted through her foggy consciousness, did she realize that the car had stopped and she was being spoken to.

"Did you miss the bus, too, Lauralee?" Mrs. Newton

asked with genuine sympathy in her tone.

Lauralee's head jerked up and her long eyelashes blinked rapidly. Lapping up the sympathy like a hungry kitten after cream, she gave an almost teary nod in reply.

"Well, so did Bud," smiled the small, red-headed lady behind the wheel. "Hop in and ride along with us."

"Oh, thank you." The words tumbled out breathlessly as she bolted through the open door and sat down beside Bud in the back seat.

Bud greeted her with a lazy wave of a hand and a "Hi" that got mixed up with a wide yawn and came out unintelligible gibberish.

"Hi, yourself," Lauralee replied, just as casually. She sank back thankfully against the pale blue plastic-covered seat. One of the sheets of printed matter slid from her clutch and fluttered to the floor.

"Oh, dear," she said and hastily bent over to retrieve it. Bud reached for it, too, and they bumped heads.

"I'm sorry," she said in confusion. Then she sat back and clamped her lips tight and took a hard grip on the rest of her school material. She was grimly determined not to move a single muscle the rest of the way to school—for if she did, with her luck, something would happen to break this brief spell of good fortune that had come to her.

It wasn't that she was self-conscious around Bud—she had known him much too long for that.

The Newtons lived just around the corner from the Larkins, in a big, rambling white frame house on Fremont Avenue. She and Bud had started to kindergarten together and had progressed, in a relation of mutual tolerance, through the lower grades. They hadn't liked each other especially but they hadn't hated each other either.

Lauralee had never had much regard for any boys—Binky and her father excluded, of course. In fact, she and Jenny had felt nothing but scorn for other girls who dissolved in giggles and coy mannerisms the minute a boy came into view.

Years ago, when she had been in grade school, she and Jenny had played ball with the boys in the vacant lot behind their house. But since they had stopped that, both girls had considered boys pretty much of a nuisance. She *still* thought so and she was certain Jenny did, too.

At least that was what she tried to think. But lately Bud had taken to coming over to her house and they talked in a brotherly-sisterly fashion. Sometimes he sprawled in a chair in the recreation room of the Larkin house and they watched the Chicago Cubs or White Sox games on TV, saying very little to each other. He drank quantities of Cokes and other soft drinks her mother would bring down as well as cookies, popcorn, and other goodies.

"You'd think he never had a square meal at home," Mr. Larkin would sometimes snort. Of course they knew that wasn't true for Mr. Newton owned a prosperous restaurant and they had plenty to eat.

"Growing boys"—Mother would smile because she liked Bud—"need lots of food."

"If that boy grows any taller he'll go right through the roof."

"Yeah," Binky was fond of adding, "what Bud needs is shrink food."

It was all in fun, of course. So far as Lauralee was concerned, they could say what they liked. She regarded Bud as just another one of those expendables, boys. And besides, she had a suspicion he came over to her house to get out of doing chores around his own.

It became tiresome, too, listening to Bud sigh for the car he was going to get when he was old enough to get a driver's license. He was practically counting the days until then, it seemed.

"Well, I think Bud is just *darling!*" Maxine would say, not understanding her attitude at all.

Lauralee wished her sister could see Bud this morning, eyes blurred with sleepiness and shoulders drooping like a tired hounds'. She wouldn't think he was so darling.

Lauralee couldn't understand why any girl should go all coy and giggly around *him*. He was a woman-hater anyhow. He had told her so several times during the last few weeks. She knew, though, that it was just a blind to cover the torch he still carried for Eloise Fisher.

Eloise was the kind of girl that boys carried torches for! She had auburn hair, fair skin, and big blue eyes with lashes that could flutter boys into a happy daze.

During their last year in junior high school Bud had spent pockets of money on sodas and such for that pretty redhead. They had been known as the Indestructible Pair. But that was before Robert Lee Morton had drifted up from Alabama, right after school was out for the summer, and Eloise had given Bud the air so fast he was still reeling.

"Ah dew declaih!" Bud had exclaimed one afternoon as he sat on the Larkin front steps discussing his latest lawn-mowing job—he got paid in cash money for *it*—when Robert and Eloise strolled by, holding hands. "The Sowth is rahsing agin!"

He had snorted so loudly that Robert Lee had turned and said grimly, "Want to make something of it?"

And Eloise had fairly purred at being fought over by two men. All of which Lauralee had viewed with scornful disgust.

Bud had subsided then, of course. When the pair had passed, he had pulled himself up and, with all the scorn at his command, had snorted, "Women! I wouldn't be caught dead with one!" And he had stalked off home.

He had come back a little later, however, and eaten four of the chocolate brownies Mother had said she was baking.

The silence in the back seat was thick this morning as Mrs. Newton turned onto Maple Avenue, the main shopping street of the suburb. Down through the business section of Elm Park they went—Lauralee staring unseeingly out one side of the car and Bud out the other—then over the North Western tracks and past the station and around on Graham Street.

They were nearing the high school now. Groups of boys and girls, who lived near enough to walk to school, were strolling down the walks. Lauralee's interest picked up. Was there someone among them that she knew? Someone who would see her and wave and she could wait for outside the front door of the building? She craned her neck. Not one familiar face did she see. She settled back, hopelessly.

Bud bounced back, too, against the seat, his face beet-red with anger.

"Looks like she cut her hair with a pencil sharpener!" he growled. Then Lauralee saw the auburn tresses passing beneath a maple tree, vying in color with some of the turning leaves. Eloise! And beside her was Robert Lee Morton— tall, and with dark, waving hair cut in a sort of modified Roman emperor style—leaning close.

How much nicer his haircut looked than Bud's brush cut, short and standing straight up like the crest of a jaybird. And Eloise's pert, gamin hairdo blended perfectly with her impish personality.

Lauralee sighed. Girls like Eloise and Max never felt lonesome or lost, as she did that morning. If only she had a wee bit of their looks, bounce, and blithe spirits.

She was past hope in that department, Lauralee was sure. No sense in her trying to keep up with the latest in hair styles and fads in clothes. On her they'd look ridiculous rather than chic. Jenny had felt the same way.

The blue sedan edged its way through a swarm of boys and girls clustered about the entrance to the grounds and then swept around the curving driveway that led to the big, wide, double doorway of Willowlake Community High School.

"Oh, thank you, Mrs. Newton!" Lauralee said as she opened the door and tumbled out.

"See you," Bud said to his mother, and did the same. Then he loped off toward Sammy Taylor, an old buddy, who waved an arm at him from beside the entrance.

Lauralee found herself all alone. It wasn't that she didn't know any of the young folks who drifted about like gently falling leaves. Here and there she saw a familiar face and remembered the name of its owner. But she'd feel foolish hailing any of them.

It was early, the blue sedan having taken a more direct route to school than the bus would. Lauralee found herself wishing the bus would hurry and come. Tammy Taylor would be on it, and Susan Adams, Tiny's sister. She knew *them* well enough to hail, though they wouldn't have much to say to her nor she to them. She had never tried to get really acquainted with them, never having had any need for their friendship. She and Jenny had been so close.

She sat down on the cement steps, feeling curious eyes upon her and thinking others were talking about her forlorn look. She tried to look busy with her cards and schedules and booklet, reading over lines she already knew by heart.

Bits and snatches of the gay chatter of others came to her.

"Oh, what a cute dress! Where did you get it?"

"My mother made it!"

"I wish I had a mother who could make such dream clothes."

"I said to Johnny. . . ."

"Tom called last night and he asked me to go to the show at the Tivoli with him Saturday night."

"I love your new hairdo."

"Put it up myself—on rollers."

Lauralee looked up in time to see a slender, smiling girl whirl so all could admire her hairdo, fore and aft.

"That's for me," she thought wryly. "I'd look like I had a beehive on my head." Her gaze flicked over to a cluster of boys. Their talk ran more to sports and who would make this or that team this year. Bud Newton's name was mentioned frequently by the boys.

Bud, standing on the fringe of the group, took it all with a quiet grin. He had played basketball and baseball in junior high, reaching star status in both. During summers he had been a leading light in both Little League and Pony League. But he wore his honors lightly and with good grace, not letting them go to his head or put a swagger in his manner as some boys did.

Eloise Fisher had liked going around with such a big wheel. She liked being seen with outstanding fellows. That had been her reason for switching to Robert Lee. Besides being tall and rangy and athletic-looking, he was downright handsome in a rugged, outdoorsy way. And that accent! The soft, slow drawl enchanted the other girls, too. Several had set their caps for Robert Lee.

"A real dreamboat," they had murmured ecstatically.

That in itself was a challenge to Eloise. She had fluttered her lashes and cooed and gushed in what she thought was a Belle from Birmingham manner. Anyway it worked. It wasn't long before Bud knew that he and his soda money were no longer as attractive to Eloise as they had been.

"Dumb bunny, Bud!" Lauralee and Jenny had aired their opinions frankly. "He thinks Robert Lee rode up on his white charger and *took* Eloise away from him!"

The other girls in the class had been chagrined at the swiftness with which Robert Lee had been taken out of circulation. Eloise could have given them a chance, especially since she was already going with Bud.

Lauralee and Jenny had watched the little drama with scornful indifference. They felt no need for the company of boys; they had each other. . . .

Eloise and Robert Lee came into view then. They drifted apart casually and soon Robert Lee was being welcomed by the group of boys of which Bud was a part. He and Bud were talking as though they had never had a difference in their lives. That was the way Bud was, easygoing and never carrying a grudge, or at least not letting it show.

Eloise walked toward Eileen Thompson and Marion Avery, her chums when no boys were around. They greeted her cheerfully, not seeming to resent any of the newcomer's winning ways with the boys. She often got dates for them, with boys she wanted to keep dangling in case of an emergency.

The three girls had been friends since kindergarten days. At the beginning of each semester they had fought to get seats near one another in homerooms, and usually succeeded. They were friendly, outgoing girls and, though they formed a tight little clique and shared secrets they wouldn't share with others, they didn't exclude others as Lauralee and Jenny had.

They turned now and waved at Lauralee. Her heart leaped. Would they ask her to join them? They didn't, for their attention was turned elsewhere.

Lauralee's disappointment was sharp. A lot she cared, she thought as she busied herself again with her sheaf of printed material. She wouldn't force herself on them, she decided.

A second later she looked up, just in time to see Elena Sloshek move in on Eloise and Eileen and Marion and two other girls who had joined them.

They rebuffed *her!* But then, most all the kids had been cool to Elena ever since the day, two years ago, when she had first come to Elm Park Junior High.

"She looks like she had just got off the boat!" the other girls had giggled and given the shy, obviously-hungry-for-friends newcomer a wide berth.

Elena had never given up, apparently not realizing how different she was from the others, with her dark hair worn in huge braids wound about her head, her humble manner, and her badly fitting clothes.

Her whole world was different from the others, too. Mr. Sloshek was employed as a gardener for the Leslie Cramers, one of the oldest and most aristocratic families of Elm Park. The Cramers' mansion, set on a spacious tree-shaded lawn, had always been a showplace, but never quite so much so as it was now that Mr. Sloshek cared for its gardens and lawn.

Mrs. Sloshek worked in a local bakery in the kitchen, though at times the kids saw her behind the counter when they stopped in to buy sweet rolls or something. The family lived in a very old house near the railroad tracks.

Lauralee had occasionally seen Mr. and Mrs. Sloshek at school affairs and noted that they always sat by themselves, stiffly, with work-worn hands folded, staring straight ahead. She had been glad each time that they weren't *her* parents.

As though accustomed now to cool indifference from her classmates, Elena walked away from the otherwise friendly group. But Lauralee knew that, like a friendly puppy, Elena would try again. In that way the dark, rather swarthy-looking girl was different from her parents.

Steeped in Old World ways of class consciousness, they kept to themselves, never trying to push.

This morning Lauralee felt a tiny stir of sympathy for Elena. They were in the same lonely boat. "I could go over and talk to her," Lauralee thought, for she knew Elena would welcome the attentions of anybody. But she didn't. That would make her feel more conspicuous than ever.

"If Jenny were here," she thought, "I wouldn't have this problem. We would be carrying on our own private conversation and we wouldn't care whether anyone else noticed us or not.

"A letter." Lauralee thought and it gave her some comfort. "I'll have a letter from Jenny waiting for me when I get home."

She and Jenny had written to each other every single day since they had parted. Jenny, she had noted with something akin to satisfaction, was as lonely out there as she was here. This afternoon, Lauralee decided, she would tell Jenny of every sorry thing that had happened to her this first day of school without her.

"You'll make new friends," Mother had said. "There's no better place than school for that."

Well, a lot Mother knew about it. Perhaps when Mother had been young things would have worked out that way. Things must have been much different in those long-ago days.

Then Lauralee saw Annie David approaching, walking right toward her with something of a light of recognition in the huge, brown eyes behind the horn-rimmed spectacles. Would Annie make the first move and speak to her? A warm feeling rose within Lauralee toward the plain-faced, skinny girl whom she had scarcely noticed before, though they had been in the same class for years.

Annie wasn't avoided like Elena was but she wasn't popular either. She was a very serious student, dressed plainly and wore her straight brown hair in a bob that required only a run-through with a comb. Unadorned herself, she was a talented artist and was called upon whenever a school project called for drawings or designs. Apparently content in her own pursuits she never tried hard to mix as Elena did. Lauralee knew she could talk to Annie without everybody turning and staring.

Suddenly Annie seemed to change her mind, if indeed she had ever intended to speak to Lauralee. Smiling shyly at nobody in particular she swerved and walked in another direction.

What a way to act! Lauralee felt she had been snubbed. Well, it would be a long time before she spoke to Annie!

Then she saw Helen Farley, another—well, sort of loner, Lauralee thought. Helen passed her, too, with only a flicker of an eyelid to reveal the fact that she had ever seen her before. And there was Daisy— In her aloneness Lauralee found herself playing a game of fitting names to girls in the crowd.

There were few enough of them that she knew. Of the many obvious freshmen—you could tell them by the copies of *Know Your Willowlake Community High School* booklets they carried—only a few, it seemed, came from Elm Park Junior High. The many others had come from Salt Creek, or Lomax, or Madison Junior Highs.

At that moment a big orange school bus pulled up in front of the school. It was greeted with squeals from girls and shouts from boys who recognized some of its passengers.

Lauralee regarded it indifferently. Then the boys and girls tumbling out told her it was the one she had missed that morning. There were Maxine and Tiny and Tammy and Susan and Jim Talbot. She knew all of *them!* Surely they would. . . .

Like a thirsty desert traveler hastening toward a cool oasis with a well in the center, she plunged in that direction.

"Max!" she called, and waved as frantically as if she hadn't seen her sister in years and never expected to see her again.

Maxine heard her and sent a casual wave in her direction. Then, her attention directed elsewhere, she apparently forgot all about Lauralee. She was soon surrounded by other girls and swept away.

Lauralee's buoyed-up spirits blooped. If Maxine had betrayed her and doomed her to the stake, she couldn't have felt more abandoned. Dejectedly she watched her sister's retreating figure.

Gay, carefree, popular Maxine, to whom everything nice happened, to whom everything came so easily. Why, after all, should she bother with a lonely younger sister?

The bell rang then and, like dust into a vacuum, the boys and girls surged through the open doors. Lauralee was carried along, willy-nilly, not having the slightest idea where she was going. In spite of this, a feeling of happiness welled up within Lauralee. She was in school again. And she had always liked school. She'd get along somehow, friendless and alone though she was!

3

A Serious Problem

First she must get her bearings, find out where she was going. Everyone else seemed to know his or her destination and the shortest way to it, but she didn't.

Her booklet. That would tell her. Lauralee stopped and, using her elbow as a sort of battering ram, she made her way to one wall of the corridor. She flattened herself against it and opened her copy of *Know Your Willowlake Community High School*. On the map she sought the location of her locker. Frowning, she tried to trace the route she had taken on registration day.

Larkin . . . L. That was the section her locker was in. Number 206, Section L.

Where was Section L? There was A and K and O and— she began to think that finding L on that map was akin to locating a cork on the waters of the ocean. Vaguely she remembered her locker being close to a science classroom. Through an open door she had distinctly seen vials and tubes and equipment that told her so.

"Having trouble, fair one?" a warm, friendly, masculine voice murmured over her shoulder.

Her head went up and turned and, though her vision was a bit blurred from peering at the map, she saw a nice-looking boy of seventeen or so smiling at her.

A sudden fluttery feeling rose within her and she was horrified by it. He was *so* attractive! Desperately she tried to hide her feelings. Mustering every effort to appear indifferent and nonchalant, she replied evenly, "Yes, I am. I'm trying to figure out where the L locker section is."

His grin was most ingratiating. And, in spite of her efforts to control the growing pleasure his attentions gave her, she thought how different he was from the rough, unmannerly boys she had known in junior high. Or had she changed? It was so confusing.

Then again, perhaps this was one of the rewards of growing up. If so, then high school was going to be all right.

He murmured, "Perhaps I can help you." And gently but firmly he took the booklet from her and looked at the map, his tanned face puckered in thought. Suddenly snapping his fingers with a flourish, he indicated the stairs that turned off to the right of them.

"Right up there," he said gallantly, "and turn to the left. Down that hall to the end and to the right. You'll find your locker section there, between a science and a home ec room!"

"Oh, thank you!" Lauralee cried gratefully. Taking back her booklet she started in the direction he had indicated. Up the stairs she went, her flats happily tapping to the tune of her rising spirits.

Now her senses fairly reeled with joy at the old, familiar smells of new books, fresh paint and the tang of the autumn air that came through the big open window at the first landing. Her step springy, she thought how wonderful it was to be back in school. She had always liked school. Summer was all right, with its lazy, no-schedule days, but one did tire of the meaningless emptiness. The months ahead, even without Jenny, promised now to be full to the brim with important, stimulating activities.

Reaching the top of the stairs, she distinctly heard a voice say in passing, "Hi, Lauralee." It was Annie David, smiling at her shyly as she went down the stairs.

The tone of Lauralee's voice would indicate they had been friends of long standing. "Annie! How wonderful to see you," she cried, and at the moment she meant it.

"Nice to see you, too." And Annie was gone, swallowed up by the flowing stream of boys and girls hurrying here and there. The brief encounter sent Lauralee's bubbling spirits a bit higher. Willowlake didn't seem to be the cold, impersonal place she had expected. It would soon become, she thought now, as dear and familiar as Elm Park Junior High had been.

Now, where had that nice boy told her to go? Oh, yes, turn to the left. She turned to the left. Down that hall to the end. She went down the hall. Then turn right. She turned right, and went through a door and found herself on a balcony, looking down into the school auditorium!

She turned to go back. "I made a wrong turn somewhere," she muttered, half-aloud.

"Oh, no, you didn't," came a voice from beside her. "That grinning goon sent you up here on purpose, too."

She whirled and saw a short, thin boy with a disgusted expression on his rather sharp features. In his hand was the familiar booklet, the freshman badge.

"You mean. . . ?" She was bewildered.

"Big-shot senior having fun," the boy snorted as he turned and stalked out. "Some joke. Ha, ha, ha."

"But he couldn't!" Lauralee wailed.

Another freshman came in, a plump girl with a round baby-doll face and enormous blue eyes. Disappointment was written all over her trusting features. All that smooth politeness had been nothing but a big sham!

Another freshman came in, and another. Of all the mean tricks! If that boy with the silly grin had been near Lauralee then she would have flattened him with her handbook. The big oaf!

Lauralee's spirits went down as fast as they had gone up. Misty-eyed with disillusionment, she went back into the hall and looked around. Harried and bewildered freshmen were everywhere. How anyone could have taken such a mean advantage of them was beyond her. What a creepy place this school was, anyway.

But she had known all along it would be. Now where *was* her locker? She shuddered. Four years she would have to spend here.

Again she took out her map and studied it. Nobody would distract her this time. At almost the first glance she found the section marked L lockers. It was on the second floor, directly down the corridor from where she was now, on the opposite side of this wing of the building.

She marched down the corridor, looking neither to the right nor the left.

Section L. . . . There it was. Passing the science room she

had remembered, she stopped before locker 206.

Now where had she written down the combination? Oh, yes, on one of the information sheets. She leafed through them and finally found it.

"If I get to my first class before noon I'll be doing well," she mumbled as she turned the handle first one way and then another. The locker opened.

What class came first? She had practically memorized her schedule before she had left home, but she had completely forgotten it now. She found the schedule sheet. Oh, yes, Latin! She grabbed her Latin book. Another bell rang. She had just three minutes to get there. Again she consulted her map. Latin was in Room 310. Where was 310? On the next floor almost directly above where she was now.

Paying no attention to the chatter about her, she turned and hurried down the hall and up another stairway to the third floor. She ran down another corridor, the white frosted glass of the doors she passed seeming like rails of a picket fence. At last—Room 310. With a sigh of relief she went through the door and slid into a front seat, just as another bell rang.

Mrs. Meyer, the Latin teacher, sat at her desk at the front of the room. Plump, rosy-cheeked and smiling, she had a manner as crisp as the tailored, green-checked cotton dress she wore.

"Good morning," she said to Lauralee, nodding in a friendly way.

"Good morning," replied Lauralee, her faded spirits reviving.

She knew at once that she and Mrs. Meyer were going

to get along fine. That was important to her. She was a good student, though she had to work for her grades, but it seemed she could work harder for some teachers than for others.

Mrs. Meyer was neither gushy nor reserved. She would tolerate no nonsense, but you would always know where you stood with her. Lauralee liked such teachers, for as a rule they played no favorites.

Of course, if she were like Maxine and could make good grades without half trying, it would be different. Quickly she pushed that depressing thought to the back of her mind. She had enough to contend with without that.

She looked around. Where was everybody? Only two other students had arrived, a boy and a girl and she knew neither of them.

"It is always like this the first day," Mrs. Meyer smiled. "But tomorrow the first-year students will have their bearings and will be here on time."

And tomorrow, Lauralee suspected, any tardy pupil had better have a good excuse! That was the way Mrs. Meyer would be, tolerant up to a point but beyond that . . . zzzzt!

Mrs. Meyer greeted two other students who stumbled, dazedly, into the room. Expecting a reprimand, they were greeted with a smile but told that she presumed they knew the location of the room now. Others came straggling in, some breathless from rushing. Lauralee recognized the plump girl she had seen on the balcony. But the plump girl apparently didn't recognize her. Well, I won't bother to smile at her again, Lauralee vowed. Who did that girl think she was anyway?

Unconsciously she watched for someone she knew to come in. And someone did—a tall, darkly handsome lad with a Roman emperor haircut.

"Ah'm sorry Ah'm late," he apologized politely.

"That's quite all right," Mrs. Meyer replied, and Lauralee could tell she was making an effort not to smile too obviously at the southern drawl. "Tomorrow you will know how to get here, won't you?"

"Yes, ma'am."

Like a magnet Robert Lee Morton drew the eyes of everyone in the room—everyone, that is, except Lauralee. She was watching with extreme disgust the expressions of adoration that spread across the faces of several of the girls. How silly some girls acted the minute an attractive boy appeared!

Then, without meaning to, she sent a hurried glance in his direction. Her breath caught in her throat. He *was* handsome and, best of all, apparently completely unaware of it. He caught her eye, grinned, and winked slowly. She jerked her gaze away, blushing furiously. The big oaf!

Was that a titter she heard from behind her?

Her back stiffened and she sat up straight as a ramrod. Lowering her chin, she looked down at the book on her desk and determined *never* to look at that boy again!

She passed the rest of the period in a miserable state of self-consciousness, the back of her neck burning from the mocking eyes she was sure were on her. When Mrs. Meyer called the roll and each pupil stood, so the teacher could familiarize herself with each one, Lauralee almost forgot to answer to her own name. And that caused more titters.

She could have squealed for joy when the bell rang

signifying the end of *that* class. Once again in the corridor she searched for the location of Study Hall 1.

This time, she decided grimly, she would find it without any help from anybody, and she did.

She filed into the hall with a large group of students, so many that she was sure she would not see one that she knew. Not that she cared if she didn't. From now on she would be a loner, go her own way, and not care whether she spoke to anyone or anyone spoke to her. She would be safe from embarrassment then. The others would call her a square when she wasn't around to hear, and smile and ridicule her queer ways. But she wouldn't care.

Finding a seat, she opened her Latin book. Mrs. Meyer had given them a lot of homework for the first day, it seemed to her. She had heard from Max and others that the teachers at Willowlake made regular work horses of the students, and they were right, she concluded. But that was fine with her. It would keep her busy and her thoughts occupied, so that nothing else would matter. She would make good use of the study period every day by doing her Latin assignment. She wouldn't be popular and have lots of friends like Max, but she would make good grades.

She began to conjugate a Latin verb . . . *amo, amas, amat.* . . . But, in spite of her firm resolution of a minute before, her eyes slid around the room past two unfamiliar faces and then ran right into the big, brown eyes of Elena Sloshek, which lit up immediately.

Quickly Lauralee dropped her own gaze back to her book. That foreign-looking girl needn't think she was going to be a friend of hers!

Friend! Oh, if that were only Jenny sitting over there! Thoughts of the many miles that lay between her and her only true friend sent her spirits into a real tailspin.

She sighed silently, and caught a glimpse of Eileen Thompson three rows over. Was Eloise far away? She couldn't see the pretty redhead, but she did see Bud! Her heart gave a tiny leap. She yanked it back quickly. He was just a pesty boy and interested *only* in Eloise anyway. Still, the sight of the back of his familiar head with its crew cut and close-set ears—a nicely shaped head she had to admit— was comforting. But beside him sat that perfectly awful Robert Lee Morton!

Both of them just sat there, grinning at all the girls who came by—so sure of themselves and the power they had over women. That was boys for you, always thinking they were fortune's gift to the girls. Well, she wasn't going to have anything to do with any of them, that Robert Lee Morton in particular. Eloise Fisher could have him and welcome.

Now, how had she got to thinking about boys? Hastily she went back to her Latin verbs.

Two classes later she found herself in front of Robert Lee, in the line before the counter in the cafeteria. She had her plate of spaghetti and meat balls on her tray and was just picking up her salad and glass of milk and gelatin dessert when she noticed him.

He grinned at her and winked again. And again that flustered, fluttery feeling took over. How could she be so silly? Just because that horrid boy acknowledged the fact that she was alive? She answered with a small, tight grin and hurried through the check-out.

Embarrassment again made her feel as awkward as a fish out of water. Why? Then she knew. If Jenny had been with her it would never have happened. They would have been chattering so they wouldn't have noticed if Rock Hudson were behind them. It was her being alone and friendless that made her easy prey to such feelings. Well, she'd be careful from now on to give Mr. Morton a wide berth.

Once through the check-out she hunted desperately for an empty chair at one of the long tables, just *one* chair. She didn't want him following and sitting beside her.

There it was, a lone empty chair, in a long line of chattering girls. What did they have to talk so much about? Cheeks pink and eyes downcast, she put distance between herself and that smart aleck Southern boy.

She put her tray before her on the table. Then she caught a glimpse of him making his way to a table of yakking boys. Well, she hoped he didn't think she wanted him to follow her!

The girls, all strangers to her, looked at her briefly and then went back to their chattering. Sophomores, most of them, they seemed to know each other intimately. Clothes, boys, boys, clothes, those were the things they talked about.

Lauralee ate in silence, every bite as tasteless as sawdust. How could she have ever thought she would like it here at Willowlake?

The long day ended with a combination homeroom and study period. With a desperate anxiety Lauralee made her way to it. She took one look at Mr. Lawton, a boyish-looking man, and decided she wasn't going to like him at all. "He tries so hard to be jolly and gay," she thought with annoyance, "and how he favors the boys!"

She sat down glumly. Frankly critical, she surveyed the other members of her homeroom class, with whom she would likely spend her entire high school career.

Elena sat not far away. She would! And there were Eileen Thompson and Bud and—oh, no, Robert Lee Morton!

With fiendish glee she wondered what would happen if Eloise Fisher walked in. But the flirty Miss Fisher had evidently been assigned to another homeroom. When the door closed she wasn't there.

Lauralee turned and looked around. Annie, who sat in the back row, nodded and smiled. Lauralee gave a tiny wave of her hand and turned back to the front, not at all sure she wanted Annie for a friend either. Annie was a square, and had been the subject of many jokes all through junior high.

Well, she was planning on becoming a square, too, wasn't she?

Still— Well, to tell the truth, she didn't know what she wanted, except to have Jenny sitting there beside her. A tear squeezed out of the corner of her eye.

It was then that Mr. Lawton handed her a mimeographed paper and said, "Lauralee, will you read the bulletin for me? Now, boys and girls, give this your close attention. Then you won't have to ask about each announcement later."

Lauralee gulped and stood up. She was so nervous that the paper in her hand shook, though she didn't know one good reason why she should be.

There were several announcements—about dates and places of meetings of the various school clubs, about a couple of new school rules, a white cashmere sweater that had been found on registration day, and the athletic coach's directions for the scrimmages being held. Reading slowly Lauralee tried to keep the waver out of her voice. Did anyone suspect how much her knees shook?

"A little louder, please," Mr. Lawton smiled at her. "We want those in the rear row to hear."

Lauralee raised her voice and was horrified at the squeaky sound she heard. She'd have to get better control of herself than this. Then, looking up, as she had been told to do when reading, she saw Robert Lee Morton looking straight at her!

She felt faint.

"Saturday evening, the twenty-first of September"—the squeak got infinitely worse—"the Music Club will give a dance in the cafeteria honoring all incoming students. Please come." She sat down with a plump. Mr. Lawton indicated he wanted the bulletin returned and Lauralee got up to return it to him. As she did so she brushed against her Latin book, and all the other books and papers and pamphlets stacked on the arm of her chair flew in all directions.

If only the floor could have swallowed her then!

As though that weren't bad enough, it was Robert Lee and Mr. Lawton who helped her pick up the things and stack them back where they had been. Robert Lee grinned like a Cheshire cat all the time. She could have smacked him!

She knew that her cheeks were flushed, her hair awry, and a big smudge adorned her forearm.

All around her she heard titters and chatter. At first Lauralee was sure all of it was directed at her. Then she heard the word, "Dance," and realized the excitement was over the event she had just read about.

The first big social event of their high school career, that was what the Music Club Dance would be! A date dance! So much more grown-up than the junior high affairs where the boys and girls had arrived separately and then danced together.

The boys would escort the girls to this dance. They would be paired off from the minute they left home until they returned.

The same thought ran through the minds of all the girls. "Will a boy ask *me?*"

"Well," thought Lauralee grimly, "that's no serious problem for me. No boy will ask me and if he does I won't go with him."

4

A Wacky Idea

This *laugh, clown, laugh* bit wasn't at all funny, Lauralee concluded. Ever since she had arrived home and had
passed the small sewing room upstairs in which her mother
was busy, she had been forcing a smile and answering, "Fine,
oh, fine," to all sorts of questions about her first day at
school. By dinner time her jaws ached and her voice
rasped from the falsely cheerful note she had injected into
it.

She was placing the silver on the table in the dining
room when Dad went through the hall and stopped in the
doorway and asked, "How did my girl get along her first
day in high school?"

Well, she just couldn't let him down, not after the way
she had acted that morning anyway. So she raised her head,
faced him squarely, smiled brightly, and replied, "Fine,
oh, just fine."

"That's good," Dad replied and was gone to the kitchen
to indulge in his exasperating habit of snatching things to
eat from the various platters and bowls Mother was filling.
Talk about bulb snatchers, Dad and Binky were the worst

food snatchers in the business.

"By the time I get the dishes on the table," Mother often wailed, "there isn't any food left in them."

Dad would grin and reply, "Well, you and Maxine said you were dieting."

"But we aren't planning on starving, Father!" Maxine would remind him. They always called him *Father* when they reprimanded him. Otherwise it was Dad or Pop.

As Dad disappeared, Lauralee's smile faded. Even Jenny's letter had been a disappointment. It had sounded almost cheerful! Several times Jenny had mentioned a girl named Wanda, as though she were trying to tell Lauralee gently that she had, or was about to have, another friend. Not one word did she say about missing Lauralee or wishing she were back in Elm Park.

How could Jenny forget so easily? The thought fairly trembled in her mind. *She* never would.

Soon everybody was seated and, as usual, the events of the day were discussed. Lauralee told about the boy misdirecting freshmen on purpose, but she didn't say she was one of them. She knew Binky. He'd just up and ask her how she could be so dumb? And the others would probably think it was a big joke.

Lauralee was glad when the talk turned from her to Maxine.

"Oh, most of the kids from last year are back," Maxine said, very conscious of her new dignity as a senior, "and I met our two new foreign exchange students. They are darling."

Maxine started to slather butter on a roll, then decided

against it and began to eat it plain.

"Who are they? Where are they from?" Mrs. Larkin asked, always interested in such things. She took a very active part in P.T.A. and last year had served on committees in the grade school, junior high, and high school organizations. This year she was on the executive board of the high school P.T.A. and Max and Lauralee were very proud of her. It was nice to know your parents were really interested in school affairs, though sometimes, like this afternoon, Lauralee had thought they could be *too* interested.

"Jennie Matsuko is from Japan and she looks like one of those adorable little dolls in a kimono," Maxine bubbled enthusiastically, "only she dresses just like us, and Mary Kelly is from Ireland and, while she is a little on the buxom side, she is darling, too."

"And I think it's just darling that you think they're just darling!" chortled Binky. Max stuck out her tongue at him and Mother frowned at both.

"Well, how do they like it here?"

"They say they are crazy about it," Max buttered a roll this time and looked at it so long and lovingly it made the others fidgety, "but they are puzzled at some of our customs."

"Like what?" asked Dad.

"Well, Jennie thought it was awful funny when her family, the Watsons with whom she is living here, were driving her back from New York, and *Mrs. Watson* picked out the motel where they were to stay for the night."

"What was so funny about that?" asked Mother.

Maxine shrugged. "Well, she says in her country the

father makes all such decisions and nobody questions his authority even a teeny bit."

This threw Binky into hysterics. Honestly, boys could be the silliest things, Lauralee thought, eying him disgustedly. Imagine *him* growing up with authority!

"And that," said Father, "sounds like a most excellent custom."

"Well, anyway," Max finished, "we're all going to help them get accustomed to our ways."

Dad rolled his eyes ceilingward and said in mock horror, "Heaven forbid."

That was the very first laugh Lauralee had had all day. Though Dad could be pretty corny sometimes, he could be amusing, too. And besides she was glad they were discussing something besides *her* day.

Mother turned to her then and said pleasantly, "And a week from Saturday you will be going to the Music Club Dance, won't you? I'm making a lovely dress for you to wear."

She might have known. She couldn't even suffer in privacy. Lauralee looked down at her plate and mumbled, "I'm not going to that dance."

Mother's brows shot up. "Not going?" she echoed.

"Why not?" demanded Dad. "Max here—"

Lauralee looked up quickly, tears stinging her lids. There it was, comparing her to Maxine again. Mr. Larkin clamped his lips together and did not finish his remark.

But the damage had been done. Lips trembling, Lauralee whispered, "Nobody's asked me."

"Boo hoo!" sniffed Binky.

"Leave the table, young man," said Father sternly. Binky left. He was finished with dinner anyway, and it was easy to see he was glad to go.

"But it's early yet," Maxine said soothingly, adding cannily, "Besides, there are ways of getting a boy to ask you."

Lauralee shot her a surprised look.

"Do you get dates that way?" she demanded.

Maxine shrugged. "Let's just say that I see to it I'm not left out of anything. What's the matter with Bud?"

"Nothing." Lauralee rose and asked to be excused. She stopped in the doorway. "But you don't think I'd let him know I want him to take me to a dance, do you?"

Play second fiddle to Eloise Fisher? She guessed not!

Lauralee walked slowly up the stairs to her room. This was not her night to clear the table and rinse the dishes and she wasn't going to risk being drawn into the job.

It depressed her to think that she would probably have to get a boy to ask her to that dance, as Maxine had suggested. Her parents never wanted their children to miss out on anything. And if she were going to keep, even halfway, in her parents' good graces. . . . She sighed. Pleasing parents sometimes took a bit of doing.

Going into the room she shared with Max she shut the door firmly behind her, glad of a few minutes all to herself—to brood. But, as usual, after a few minutes of it the things she brooded about didn't seem worthy of the effort. When Maxine came up she had written a letter to Jenny, trying to leave out the grimmer parts of the day, as she was sure now her friend had done.

Next day around the lockers she heard several freshmen

girls discussing the coming dance. She couldn't help but hear for she did nothing to keep from it.

To her surprise she found only one of them had a date for the coming event, with a boy she had been seeing a lot anyway.

"Nobody's going to ask *me*," said a small, dark-haired girl slamming the door of her locker, "so I'm not even thinking about going."

Lauralee watched in amazement as the speaker swung off down the hall. She was little and cute, yet she sounded just like her! Some boy would most certainly ask that little charmer even if the little charmer didn't think some boy would.

"But I'm no charmer," she wailed to herself, poking her billfold with house keys and lunch money into the back of her locker. "Besides, I can't think of one single boy I would go with anyway."

Not Bud certainly, mooning around as he always was over Eloise. Nor Robert Lee Morton, that awful clod! Of course, there were Leo Holt and Ben Thomas and maybe, just maybe, Tom Harris, though he was on the short side. She shrugged. All a girl could do was sit back and wait for one of them to ask her.

Disgustedly she slammed the door of her own locker. Well, she wasn't going to wait for some old boy to ask her to a dance, not even to please her parents. And, as for Max's suggestion—well, that might be all right for some boy-crazy girls but not for her.

She heard one of the girls giggle. "And I happen to know, from the way my twin brother talks, that most of the boys are afraid to ask girls for fear they will be turned down."

Lauralee's brows lifted. Well, that was a switch. Imagine any old boys thinking like that. With their swagger and noisy ways.

Another girl squealed, "What about our Date Pins? You know, the ones we used to wear in junior high?"

"Say, that's an idea! What do you think, Lauralee?" And to Lauralee's surprise the girls whirled toward her, questioning looks on their eager faces. Yes, there was Lila Loring who, she faintly remembered, had been in her class last year.

"Well, I, uh, it *is* an idea!"

Memories of the pins came flooding back. Lauralee remembered how scornful she and Jenny had been when the fad had spread throughout the school. It seemed as if everybody was making and wearing them, even the boys.

"I still have mine," Lila said.

"I can make another one."

That would be easy for they had been made of a bit of fine wire threaded with colored beads from the dime stores. One end had been bent into a loop and a small safety pin attached to it. With the loop worn at the top it had meant *Taken,* at the side, *Looking,* and at the bottom, *Not interested.*

Lauralee and Jenny had finally succumbed to pressure and worn them, too, with the loops at the bottom. That had been fun in an adolescent sort of way.

"But I couldn't—" She faltered now.

"Why not? What's the harm in letting the boys know we

want them to ask us to the dance?"

Lila's eyes sparkled. "Well, I'm going to wear mine in the morning just to see what happens."

"What about you, Lauralee?" another girl asked. "Are you game?"

"We-e-l-l, I don't know, maybe. . . ." Lauralee floundered in a sea of indecision, as usual. A bell rang then and broke up the group and she was glad for the time to think it over.

Suddenly it came to her how nice it had been for them to ask her opinion. Apparently Lila had forgotten how close had been the ring she and Jenny had drawn about themselves all during their years in junior high. And the other girls, having come from other schools, hadn't known her at all.

She kept thinking about the pin all day. Where was hers? In the small velvet-lined box on her dresser where she kept her pretty pins and the locket Dad had brought back from a business trip to New York?

Several times during the day she changed her mind. She would wear it—she wouldn't wear it. When she arrived home she looked in the jewel box and there it was, on the bottom. She slipped it into her Latin book.

Mother called her into the sewing room and showed her the velveteen dress she was making for her. Extremely simple lines, which Lauralee liked, earmarked all of Mother's dressmaking. This one, of a sparkling ruby-red color, had a round neck, puffed sleeves and a beautifully flared skirt. How nice it would look with a pin at the shoulder. Pin? She'd *have* to wear that Date Pin and get a date now. She couldn't disappoint her mother and not wear that dress to the dance! She just knew Mother had had that Music Club Dance in mind with every stitch she had taken on it.

Even Binky gave a long whistle and said, "Wow!" when he saw her whirl in the dress before the full-length mirror on her closet door. Though she knew he was doing it half in fun, she kept thinking it would be a shame not to wear the lovely thing.

"I'll start dinner, Mom," she cried in an expansive mood while Mother, sitting on the floor, pinned up the hem.

"Fine, then I can practically finish it this afternoon," Mother replied.

Lauralee rattled pans and peeled potatoes and browned meat and mixed biscuits for an hour or more. She was quite a good cook—even Binky sometimes ate her culinary efforts without making any smart remarks.

While she was setting the table, Dad did an elaborate tiptoe act into the kitchen and started his usual snitching. But Lauralee was pleased. He said the celery sticks tasted pretty good for an amateur cook and filched several as well as a couple of the biscuits that were her specialty.

As he went out he asked, "Are the Newtons going to drive you and Bud to the dance or shall I?"

Lauralee almost dropped a plate. How parents took things for granted!

She looked her father straight in the eye and replied, "Bud hasn't asked me to the dance."

To which he gave the exasperating reply, "*Tsk, tsk*. Boys don't have the *savoir-faire* they had when I was young."

Lauralee sighed. She'd have to wear that pin now—try to

get a date. Her parents would certainly be disappointed in her if she didn't go to that dance.

Binky, who had heard the whole thing and was pretty sharp for his tender years, turned and asked, "Want me to put a bug in old Bud's ear?"

This time Lauralee did drop a fork and it went clattering on the tile floor of the kitchen. "Don't you dare, Charles Ivan Larkin!" she cried in horror. She shuddered at the possibility.

When Mother came down, dinner was almost ready. Lauralee didn't say much while they were eating. She listened a little impatiently to the elaborate compliments her father paid her cooking with almost every bite he took and wondered whether or not she had the courage to wear that pin.

Bud came over that evening to visit with Binky. Seeing him coming through the arbor over the walk in the back yard, Lauralee turned to Binky and told him again not to mention that dance to Bud.

"Okay, okay," Binky replied patiently. "But what's the difference if I tell him you want him to take you to the dance, or you tell him by wearing that goofy pin?"

"How did you know?"

"Oh, I saw you looking at it. And I remember what you and Jenny said about it last year." Binky tapped his temple as he grinned. "Brains, that's what I'm loaded with."

Honestly, wasn't there anything she could keep secret from that brother of hers? But he was right; she had to admit it. Well, that settled it, she would *not* wear that pin.

But it was in her Latin book when she went to school

next morning. She'd just wait and see.

Lila Loring fell into step beside her as she went down the hall toward their lockers. She was wearing her pin, loop on the side.

"Where is your pin?" she asked.

"Here," Lauralee pointed to her book.

"No boy will see it there," Lila giggled.

The little dark charmer joined them, wearing her pin with the loop on the side. "Wishful thinking," she said grinning impishly and Lauralee learned her name was Myrna Lyndon.

They reached their lockers and Lauralee slipped her pin out of her book. She pinned it, loop on side, to her collar. She took a quick glance at it in the small mirror on the inside of her locker door. The bright beads winked at her. Nice, just as an ornament.

Did she actually have the courage to wear it? No. She snatched it off. A bell rang then and she started for her Latin class. Lila was right in front of her.

Leo Holt fell into step beside Lila. He pointed at the pin she wore and blurted, "Looking, Lila?"

"Sure," said Lila with a pert toss of her head, "for a boy to take me to the Music Club Dance."

Leo grinned. "Will I do?"

Lila gave him an exaggerated coy look, batted her long lashes. "Leo, this is so sudden."

Positively revolting, Lauralee thought, shuddering. But wearing the pin had worked for Lila. The velveteen dress floated before her mind's eye, as did Mother's and Dad's eager faces.

They went into the Latin room and sat down. Lila calmly turned her pin so the loop was at the top. *Taken,* it said.

Lauralee took a deep breath and pinned hers back on her collar, loop at the side. Bud passed right in front of her. He saw the pin, and his brows went up a foot.

But Lauralee bravely wore it all during class. When they filed out Bud was right behind her. Her breath came sharply. Was he going to ask her to go with him? When she thought of all the people he would make happy by doing so, herself included, she didn't see how he could do otherwise.

He walked beside her down the hall, a wide grin on his face. He pointed at the pin and his shoulders shook with silent laughter.

"Boy, has the leopardess changed her spots!" he hooted and walked on rapidly to join two other boys.

Fury rose in Lauralee, shaking her right down to the toes of her brown flats. She tore the pin from her collar, put it back into her book and a few minutes later slammed the book into her locker.

Just who had thought up that wacky idea anyhow?

5

Second Choice

Next day was Saturday. Lauralee was upstairs cleaning and straightening her side of the room she and Maxine shared.

It was a lovely day with a warm sun shining brightly. Yet it was cool, too, with a refreshing breeze drifting through the western suburbs of Chicago from off Lake Michigan. Leaves, fiery and gay as a Mexican fiesta, drifted down. Here and there neighbors were raking and burning them and the acrid smell of leaf smoke spiced the air.

Lauralee wasn't feeling gay at all. The velveteen dress hung in the closet, hidden among other things, for the sight of it brought a catch to her throat.

Boys! What sorry things they were, causing all the misery in the world. Here was that lovely dress and she couldn't wear it as Mother intended until some silly boy asked her to go with him to that dance. The thought of Bud and his ill-mannered guffaw at sight of her wearing the Date Pin still made her cheeks burn. Well, she'd, she'd. . . .

Voices drifted up from the back yard, arguing voices. Now who was that? Binky, she realized, was one of the speakers and she saw, looking out between the ruffled white curtains, that the other was Bud Newton! They were tinkering with the power lawn mower.

"Oil filter's all gummed up," said Binky. "That's why it won't start, I betcha." He wound the rope around the engine starter and pulled again. To his disgust the engine didn't even burp.

"Na, I think you're wrong, Bink," Bud said with equal conviction. "It's the spark plug. Need a new one."

To which Binky replied, "Let's take it apart and find out."

The window shot up. Lauralee leaned out.

"Don't you dare do that, Binky!" she cried. "Don't you remember how mad Dad was the last time you did that and he had to take it to a repair shop where it stayed for a week?"

Binky looked up, one lock of his unruly hair hanging in an eye. He always left it uncombed and as shaggy looking as he could so Mother would finally give her consent to a crew cut for him.

"Aw, tend to your own knittin'!" Binky snapped at her now. "I know what I'm doing."

Bud looked up. "I think he's—"

The window went down. She wasn't going to listen to anything Bud Newton had to say. She went back to her mop and the feathery dust she was chasing under her bed, contenting herself with thoughts of what Dad would say when he saw that mower lying in pieces *again* on the sidewalk.

It was Bud's fault, probably. He thought he was a mechanic, always going around taking things apart for people and being helpful in general—though his own father said he could never get Bud to lift a finger to help around home. Bud always countered that by saying the neighbors appreciated his help while his folks took it for granted. There were some who didn't appreciate it—Lauralee sniffed now.

Then her chin went up sharply. She would waste no more time thinking about Bud Newton. Did he think he was the only boy in the world? Well, she'd show him that she was no longer the unsophisticated goof she had been in junior high. She would wear that pin again Monday. Visions of three or four boys, probably seniors, asking her to the first important social event of the high school season danced like sugarplums before her. What an enchanting sight! For one brief instant she thought she could be just as popular as Max, if she tried.

She could hardly wait for Monday to come. When it did she started right out for the bus stop, bravely wearing her pin, loop at the side. Bud saw it right away and grinned like a baboon, she thought. She just gave him a languid and nonchalant "Hi," though, and let him gawk and grin.

"Don't get an idea that I want *you* to ask me," she hoped she let him know. He didn't; at least he didn't ask her.

Tammy Taylor came up then. She and Tammy had spoken to each other occasionally as they lived in the same neighborhood, but they had never been friendly. This morning, however, she greeted Tammy warmly, for Tammy was wearing a Date Pin, too, with the loop at the top! She needed the benefit of Tammy's experience.

"Who's the lucky boy?" Lauralee was determined to be lighthearted about the whole thing, even while seeking information about Tammy's date.

"Ben Thomas," Tammy giggled. Then she waved at Susan Adams approaching the corner on a run. That meant she was dismissed, Lauralee knew. Tammy and Susan had been close friends for as long as she could remember.

The bus was approaching and soon stopped before the group on the corner. Lauralee gave a gay wave of her hand to Tiny Adams, standing back politely until all the girls were on the bus, though Bud had gone on in his turn. Bud! She was better off without him.

All the way to school Lauralee tried to be gay, though she felt anything but that. Here it was Monday and the dance was Saturday and what was she going to do? All week-end she had thought that Ben Thomas might be a possibility for her date and now Tammy had taken him out of circulation.

There was still Tom Harris. "And he will come almost to my shoulder," she thought dismally. "Why do I have to be so tall?"

For a second she convinced herself that that was the reason she hadn't been besieged with calls from boys about the dance. What boy wanted to date a beanpole?

Why couldn't she have been tiny and kittenish like her sister, Max, now sitting across the aisle deep in animated conversation with Tiny Adams. And Tiny, the big goof, was lapping up the adoration in Max's looks and manner. Didn't he know she treated all boys that way? It was the way Max had of wrapping them around her little finger, treating each one as though he were the only boy in the world as far as she was concerned.

Lauralee happened to know there was really only one that Max felt that way about, Wayne Wendt. Wayne was really a big wheel in the senior class this year and he seemed to like Max, too. At any rate he called her sister often and took her to the movies occasionally.

She shrugged. Tiny would just have to find out for himself. She had her own troubles.

Tom Harris was still a possibility for her and so, of course, was Bud. Perhaps she should have let Binky drop a hint to Bud; they were together a lot. Still, she couldn't do that—let her little brother get a date for her. How desperate could a girl get?

She decided, though, that she wouldn't be so standoffish with Bud, just sort of warmly friendly and casual. No sense, really, in driving him away and then finding that Tom had asked someone else, too. That thought really did panic her.

All the way to school she was conscious of Bud and the other boys guffawing from that long rear seat. The back of her neck prickled. Were they laughing at her and the pin she was wearing, loop at side, plainly telling the world that no boy had asked her to the dance? For a fleeting second she felt like snatching it off. But she remembered the velveteen dress and didn't.

A tall, thin boy got on at the last stop and made a beeline for that back seat. "Say, Bud," he cried jovially, "I hear your old girl friend and her southern gentleman were having a bit of difference of opinion at the Pizza Palace last Saturday night!"

You could have heard a pin drop anywhere in that bus. Everybody waited for Bud's reply. When it came it was a snort that sounded loudly in the bus.

"So what! Who cares?"

Lauralee's heart did nip-ups. Was Bud finally getting over his broken romance with Eloise? If so—well, you never could tell. So far as she knew he hadn't asked anyone else, had he?

But when the school bus stopped in front of the school and Bud saw Eloise and Eileen and Marion standing beside the step, Lauralee noticed he shot the smiling redhead a tentative grin.

Eloise gave an arch toss of her bright hair as though to tell him she bore no grudge. But they did not speak—so Bud was not lost to Lauralee, yet.

There was Tom Harris, short, stocky, jolly, and lots of fun. Briefly Lauralee felt impelled to run over to him and ask him to go to the dance with her. Why not? It would end all this suspense which would be the ruination of her if it kept up much longer. Instead she walked toward him, casually, and smiled at him and said, "Hello, Tom," in a much more coy voice than she had ever dreamed she possessed.

Tom's dark head jerked her way in surprise. "Why, hello, Lauralee," he said jovially. "How's every little thing?" And he walked right past her.

At first she felt miffed by the short boy's treatment of her, but she remembered that she had never been particularly friendly to him before, so it was no wonder he was taken aback. Well, she had shown him that she wasn't so stand-offish with boys as she had once been. Maybe, just maybe, that and the sight of the pin would make him take the hint.

Myrna Lyndon came by, and she had her pin on her dress with the loop at the top, too.

"Tom Harris called me last night"—she dimpled—"and asked me to go to the Music Club Dance with him. How do you like that?"

"Wonderful!" Lauralee replied, almost choking on the word.

Now her only prospect *was* Bud! With a sinking heart she realized that he was just biding his time until the right moment came to ask Eloise. "But I won't give up hope," she vowed grimly.

All day, trying her best not to let him know, she kept her eye on Bud. She'd make him take notice of that pin. Not that he hadn't seen it; he had and he knew why she was wearing it. But all he did was grin at sight of it and that infuriated Lauralee more than ever. Biting her tongue, she kept back a couple of sharp remarks she would have liked to send his way. Who did he think he was anyway?

A girl certainly had to pocket her pride to get a boy to ask her for a date, she concluded. With longing she remembered junior high days when her life had been so much more simple. She and Jenny had never had such worries as this. Come to think of it, they had never had any worries, period—just complete bliss every hour of every day.

When school let out that day Bud was stationed out front and plainly waiting for someone. To confirm her suspicions Lauralee loitered. She saw his face light up as he turned and—yes, it was Eloise, coming out the door looking like a breath of spring morning. Eileen and Marion, as usual, were trailing in her wake.

Eloise spoke briefly to Bud, and Lauralee saw the old fatuous look spread across his tanned face when Eloise looked up at him in her familiar, flirty way as though he were the only boy in the world. She treated them all the same way, but apparently the boys didn't realize it, or didn't want to.

"I could never be that deceitful," Lauralee thought in disgust. Bud was just waiting, she knew now, for the opportunity to ask Eloise to go with him. Some boys just didn't have any pride.

Eloise's mother drove up then. The pretty redhead gave Bud a blithe wave of her hand and ran to get into the car. She motioned Eileen and Marion in with her and they drove off, leaving Bud with a silly grin on his face.

Lauralee could have stamped her foot. The dizzy dope!

"What's the matter with you?" Binky asked as he loped past her door that afternoon. "Hasn't old Bud popped the question yet?"

Lauralee made a face at him. He grinned, came back a step and looked in. "Better let me play Cupid for you, sis," he advised sagely. Then he lifted a pretend bow, pulled back an imaginary string, let an invisible arrow go and cried, "Ping!"

"Oh, *you!*" Lauralee snapped, angry and confused. She turned her back on him and started opening the letter she had taken from the hall table downstairs. Jenny had doubtless written one of her impossibly gay letters again. And it would only make her own mood grayer.

Jenny, however, was miserable, too. Her new-found friend, Wanda, had proved unreliable, having gone off with a boy when she was supposed to meet her at the library. "There will never be another friend like you, Lauralee," Jenny concluded her long letter. "Never."

"Nor you," Lauralee agreed with fervor. Holding the letter close she gazed out the window through tear-blurred eyes.

Nothing had gone right for her since Jenny had left.

The bell on the extension telephone in the upstairs hallway jolted her and, for some reason, she made a dash for it. You couldn't tell, she thought, it might be Bud. As she picked up the receiver, someone else picked up the receiver of the phone downstairs.

"Hello?" Maxine's voice was breathless, indicating to Lauralee that her sister was plainly expecting a call from Wayne Wendt. She didn't talk exactly that way to any other boy.

"Is Mrs. Larkin in?" a woman's voice asked. Lauralee and Max let out simultaneous sighs, audible only to themselves.

"I'll call her," Max replied politely.

That happened three more times before dinner was ready. Who besides Wayne would Maxine be so impatient to hear from? Then she shrugged. It *could* be others. Maxine had calls from lots of people; she was so popular.

"Mother," Max said at dinner a few minutes later, "the girls have appointed me a committee of one to hold a sort of receptionlike get-together here a week from Tuesday, the purpose being to introduce our foreign exchange students, Jennie Matsuko and Mary Kelly, around. May I?"

There was no anxiety in her manner, though, as she looked from Mother to Father. She knew she already had their permission for the party.

Mother smiled, pleased. "I think that would be splendid," she said. "We'll decorate the recreation room with paper streamers and all and you can take your record player down and dance."

Max's smile grew wider.

"We'll show them what a typical American teen-age party is like," Dad beamed. He turned to Mother. "How many Cokes and pizzas?"

"Better wait until we find out how many are coming, dear."

Nobody liked parties better than Dad, and he always made sure everybody was well fed—though along the way he usually made some wry remark about that being why his nose was so short, it was kept so close to the grindstone.

So that was settled. And Maxine had added one more feather to her social-butterfly cap. Everything turned out right for her. The party would be a rousing success, talked about for days before and after, and she would be a regular little queen at school.

Queen! Social butterfly! Giving a party to help two foreign exchange students become better adjusted to our way of life, when she had a sister who was a complete washout!

"She should take me under her wing and help me get adjusted," Lauralee wailed to herself. But she knew she wouldn't like that either. She didn't always want to be known as Maxine Larkin's sister. She wanted to be a person, respected and known in her own right.

The next day was Tuesday.

"Time marches on," Lauralee thought grimly as she

boarded the bus. Where was Bud? She looked around and saw him on the back seat, looking off into space, neither seeing nor hearing anything that went on around him.

Lauralee knew why. When the bus made its final stop, there in front of the school stood the inseparable three: Eloise, Eileen, and Marion. Bud walked straight toward them, broad shoulders thrown back, a determined look on his face.

Lauralee's eyes were sharp and so were her senses. She spied the pin on Eloise's collar, with the loop at the side, and she knew why the redhead was wearing it. She and Robert Lee were definitely on the outs and she was fishing for Bud.

She caught him quickly, too. Lauralee saw him stop and talk fast to Eloise, who turned one of her bright smiles on him and nodded. Lauralee could have cried right there for she knew that Bud had asked Eloise to the dance and Eloise had accepted! Then she saw Bud take the Date Pin on Eloise's collar and turn it around so the loop was at the top.

That was that! Her last chance to go to the dance was gone. Sadly Lauralee walked close to Eloise and Eileen and Marion. She noted that all of them wore Date Pins, loops at the top. All taken!

She smiled weakly at them. How she wished she could become a fourth in that group. They led charmed lives, just as she and Jenny had done for so long. But they didn't seem interested in her this morning, just stood there talking and laughing, without a care in the world.

Lauralee almost panicked as she saw Elena Sloshek approaching. Elena wore no pin at all. Why should she? She wouldn't be going to the dance as she had never gone to any of the social events of junior high.

Lauralee walked away quickly. "I'm not so desperate I have to run around with *her*," she thought, though it gave her small comfort.

The day seemed endless to Lauralee. She felt as gloomy as the weather looked outside the school windows—cloudy, cold and drizzly. It took Herculean efforts on her part to keep just a small portion of her mind on her school work.

How disappointed Mother and Dad were going to be in her! Maxine, the social butterfly, and she the social flop!

It was during homeroom period that it happened and Lauralee didn't really remember how. She felt somebody's eyes on her and looked around to see that it was Robert Lee Morton's. She jerked her head back. She had enough troubles without feeling him laughing at her, too.

She was on her way out of school when the southern boy caught up with her in the corridor. "What's your hurry?" he asked pleasantly enough.

Lauralee turned and saw him smiling at her in a nice sort of way. Her heart warmed toward him a little. At least for this one minute he wasn't making her feel about a quarter of an inch tall.

"Hurry? Who's hurrying?" and she took a few mincing steps. They both laughed and went on.

"Are y'all going to the dance Saturday night?" he asked in an offhand sort of way. "The Music Club thing-a-ma-jig?"

There it was! She might have known. He was trying to

embarrass her again. Well, he wasn't going to succeed this time.

"No, I'm not," she said bluntly. "Are *y'all?*"

He chuckled. "Not unless y'all go with me," was his equally blunt reply.

Lauralee flapped her lashes up and down at him. If he wanted to be funny—well, she could be funny, too.

"Y'all mean y'all want little ol' me to go with little ol' y'all?" She burst out giggling at her own silliness.

"That's just what Ah mean," he replied, and with dizzying suddenness she realized he wasn't trying to be funny!

They were outside now and, in spite of the rain, the world looked like a ball of fire to Lauralee, with bright rockets bursting every which way.

"Oh, that will be fun!" she exclaimed and hoped she wasn't wearing all her happiness on her sleeve. They parted with pleased smiles on both their faces.

On air, Lauralee walked through the doorway of her home and up the stairs to her room. She must be alone to savor for a few minutes the deliciousness of this heavenly experience.

At the door of her room she stopped, dumfounded. From behind the closed door came the sound of muffled sobs. What in the world . . . ? She opened the door and peeked in. Maxine sat up on her bed and dabbed at her eyes.

"That Wayne Wendt!" Maxine angrily answered her unspoken question. "I'll never speak to him again."

Lauralee sank down onto her own bed. "Why?" she asked softly.

"He went and asked Caroline Emery to that dance!"

Lauralee was dazed. Maxine disappointed in a date! Her favorite boy had asked someone else! It couldn't be!

"Now I won't get to go at all!" Maxine wailed. "I kept putting Tiny off waiting for Wayne and. . . ."

Lauralee shook her head slowly, trying to understand and digest this amazing news. Could it really be? She had a date with a dream boat and Max had no date at all?

Of course, she knew she was second choice—that Robert Lee had asked her on the rebound from Eloise—but it took not a whit from her feeling of satisfaction.

The telephone rang then. It was Tiny calling Maxine and asking her bluntly would she or would she not go to the Music Club Dance with him.

"Oh, why, of course, Tiny. I thought it had been understood all along." The way she said it one would have thought he was the only boy in the world for Maxine.

Lauralee rose then, happily. She got out the velveteen party dress and held it up before her at the full-length mirror. Her date wasn't the only one that was second choice!

6

The Charmed Circle

It was harder than Lauralee had thought it would be to write and tell Jenny about the Music Club Dance. How could she keep the joy she felt at being asked by Robert Lee from creeping into the telling of it?

Would Jenny think she was being disloyal? She had thought that herself about Jenny, hadn't she, when her friend had told her about Wanda?

She thought about it for quite a while, until Maxine complained about the lateness of the hour. Then she wrote hastily, "I just have to go to the silly affair. Mother and Dad would be terribly disappointed if I didn't show a little of Maxine's social sense. I hope I can enjoy it, but I won't much, because I'll be thinking of you all evening and wishing you were there with me."

Pretty good, she thought, and went on. "Remember those silly dances at junior high that our parents forced us to attend? They were riots, weren't they? The boys were so awkward and most of the girls so giggly. But at that they were more fun than this one will be . . . you were there."

The underscoring would help. Then she added, seemingly as an afterthought, "A boy named Robert Lee Morton, from below the Mason-Dixon line, has asked me to go with him. This being a date dance, I had to accept."

She ended it and read it over. Who is deceitful now? she thought. Quickly she tore the letter to shreds.

Maxine groaned, "Are you going to be up all night?"

"I'll make it short," Lauralee soothed her.

She did. She wrote about the coming dance, what a nice affair it promised to be, and how glad she was that such a sharp fellow as Robert Lee was going to be her escort.

Then she addressed and stamped it and laid it on top of her books. Creeping between the sheets, she lay back against the pillow and went blissfully to sleep.

Next morning her gaze fell on that letter. Should she mail it?

She could almost hear Jenny say, "Boy, has she changed!"

Jenny, she was sure, would never have pulled such a switcheroo in such a short time. Why, she'd probably be through high school before she woke up to the fact that boys were sort of nice, sometimes, to have around.

Jenny was the tomboyish type, not caring a hoot if she was attractive to boys or not. Her hair was cut short and most times looked as if she had combed it with her fingers. She scorned anything smacking of the sweet and girlish in clothes—her favorite outfit being ragged jeans and one of her brother's old shirts, worn outside, and saddle oxfords, preferably scuffed.

Lauralee had wanted to dress like that, casually sloppy. But Mother wouldn't let her, saying if she wore jeans around home they must be neat with a proper blouse tucked in. Even then Dad would likely take a look at her and ask Mom, "Who *is* this strange boy running around? I thought we had two daughters and one son and now I see two sons and one daughter."

He was particular about her appearance, reminding her to stand up straight and not slouch, and sometimes he twisted himself up like a pretzel in a chair to show her how she looked when telephoning.

When Robert Lee stopped by after dinner that evening to chat with her about the coming dance, she was glad she was neatly dressed. He was.

"What a nice, well-mannered boy," Mother said, pleased, after she had met him.

Dad liked the way he added, "sir" after his no's and yes's.

"Apparently doesn't hurt him to show a little respect for his elders," he added, looking straight at Binky who was forming a bad habit of answering yep and nope to questions, even those of his parents.

Binky blinked. A minute later Lauralee heard him say, "Yes, sir," to Dad, but she knew it wouldn't last.

She was glad her parents liked Robert Lee. She certainly liked being around him.

She could sense a vague change in herself. Boys, particularly Robert Lee, did not seem quite the nuisance they once had. Was she actually becoming boy-crazy like some of the other girls? Goodness, no! She was doing all this because her parents expected her to.

Deep down within her, though, she knew that wasn't true. She had never looked forward so eagerly to anything in her life as she was looking forward to that dance.

She saw Robert Lee several times the next day and he grinned at her in a special way. She replied in kind with a feeling of self-confidence she hadn't had since the first day of school.

She enjoyed, too, the feeling of indifference she had when Bud Newton was around—to be able to tell him, though not in so many words, to go fly his kite.

Once, when she knew Bud's eyes were on her, she stopped deliberately to talk to Robert Lee. She allowed herself to simper, too, until she noticed that it embarrassed Robert Lee. Then she wondered why she had put on the coy act. But she had had an impulse to show Bud that he could make a fool of himself over Eloise if he wanted to. She didn't care.

When she turned, though, and faced Bud he burst into a loud guffaw. Her ears burned. The big oaf! She gave him what she hoped was a perfectly poisonous look and, with chin held high, went on down the corridor.

After school she loitered in a rosy daze, stopping to chat with this one and that. They seemed surprised at her friend-liness. She made sure that Eloise overheard, several times, that she was going to the dance with Robert Lee. But if Eloise minded she kept it to herself.

It seemed as if nothing fazed that Eloise, thought Laura-lee. She knew only one other person who had Eloise's poise and self-confidence and that was Max. Then she remembered Max sobbing because her favorite date had asked another girl to the dance. Maybe Max wasn't so self-confi-dent. But then she saw Maxine and Wayne in an animated, friendly conversation and it was plain that Max wasn't let-ting *him* know how she felt!

"Will *I* ever be like that," Lauralee asked herself, "confident and gay no matter what?" Right now she felt that it was possible.

She missed the bus home.

"Oh, I don't care," she thought, sniffing the tangy smell of autumn and reveling in the sense of well-being the crisp air brought. "I'd rather walk home this afternoon anyway."

It was a nice day for walking and dreaming, particularly when one was in no hurry to get anywhere, and Lauralee wasn't. She strolled slowly off the school grounds, scuffing through the carpet of bright leaves and savoring the thoughts of happy times ahead.

They *would* be happy, she was sure, in spite of the fact that Jenny wouldn't be here to share them with her. The thought made her sad and depressed, but the feeling lasted only a minute, leaving with the swiftness of smoke.

Looking up for an instant, she spied a familiar-looking figure standing on the corner ahead. Vaguely she wondered who it was. Then she went on with her dreaming.

As she approached the corner the figure didn't move. She looked back but could see no one hurrying to meet the waiting person. Then the girl waved a hand in greeting. Lauralee's heart sank. It was Elena Sloshek and she was waiting for her!

Panic filled Lauralee. Of all people, she wanted least to walk and talk with that queer foreigner. Should she turn and go back, pretending she hadn't seen the wave and was returning to school for something she had forgotten? She could circle the buildings and go back around and out the rear entrance of the grounds and take that way home. It would be a longer way but almost anything would be better than sharing the company of Elena.

Her step slowed but somehow she couldn't stop it. She had reached the corner before she had thought up another solution to her problem. Elena fell into step beside her.

"Are you going my way?" Elena said shyly.

Well, which way did she think she was going? Lauralee bit back the reply. She could never be deliberately rude to anybody, so she said, "Oh, why, I suppose so. . . ."

"That is nice." Elena's English was good for she spoke slowly and carefully in her effort to make it so. Only when flustered did her speech show the influence of that spoken in her own home, some sort of Slavic tongue, Lauralee thought.

"Nice day, is it not?" Elena was determined to make the most of this sought-for opportunity.

"Ummm." Lauralee looked around, hoping that Eloise or Eileen or Marion or any of the others with whom she would liked to have been more friendly were not about. What would they think if they saw her walking home with this odd-looking person?

Lauralee was acutely conscious of the too-long skirt of her companion; the heavy, awkward shoes made for service and not for appearance, and the baggy sweater—and the ridiculous heavy braids of dark hair wrapped like towels around her head. She looked as if she had just stepped off the boat, all right.

She had, in fact, not so many years ago, as Lauralee well knew. Driven from their homeland by invading forces, the

Slosheks had been among the Displaced Persons brought to America to live.

Lauralee knew it was hard for such people to become accustomed to the more modern ways and customs of their adopted homeland. Native Americans should try to help them, she supposed. But should all the responsibility fall on her?

At the moment Lauralee was afraid it had and she didn't like it a bit. "I'll lose her the first chance I get," she vowed.

What excuse could she use? They would pass through part of the business section of Elm Park on their way. Perhaps she could stop in a store and pretend she was on an errand for Mother. She soon discarded that idea. Elena would probably go in with her and that would make them even more conspicuous.

A truck roared by. Elena waited until it had passed. "You are going to the dance of the Music Club, no?" she asked, and, in spite of Lauralee's resolve, the poignant wistfulness of Elena's voice sank deep. Somehow she hadn't thought that Elena could possibly want to go to the dance. She had never attended any of the affairs at junior high. Was she changing, too? Was she feeling now that she was in high school she would like to take a larger part in the activities going on about her?

How could that come about? One couldn't mix oil with water, unless—unless somebody took her by the hand and sponsored her. Who in the world would want to do that?

Lauralee's heart sank. She wants me to do it! Oh, no! I have enough troubles of my own.

Determination rose like a stone wall inside Lauralee.

Elena needn't think that. . . . She nodded her reply. She wasn't going to encourage Elena by getting chatty with her.

"The so-nice Morton boy asked you to go with him, did he not?" Elena seemed as determined not to lose her, conversationally or otherwise.

"Ummm." Was that one of Max's friends watching amusedly from across the street?

Elena let out a long sigh. "I wish I were going," she said softly, each word sounding as though torn from her throat. "I wish so nice a boy would ask me."

Robert Lee of the suave good looks asking Elena to a dance! The thought almost sent Lauralee to the point of giggles. But the catch in her companion's voice prevented it and the woebegone expression in the dark eyes—fringed, Lauralee noted now, with unbelievably long and heavy black lashes—melted Lauralee's resolution to have no part in Elena's troubles.

It had been so short a time since she had felt the same way; the memory was still fresh enough to hurt.

Perhaps she should help Elena. But how? She could be friendly with her. But that would certainly flatten her own chances of ever becoming a part of that charmed circle made up of the popular members of her class. Such a circle existed in every class, Lauralee knew. One group always seemed to lead, to take the most active part in every desirable activity. Maxine had always been a member of the charmed circle in her class; and now that Jenny was gone, Lauralee wanted to join the one in hers.

Even this early in the year, the circle was fast forming in the freshman class, with the leaders emerging—Bud and

Eloise, Eileen and Marion, Henry Talbot and Robert Lee, and others. Now that her own name would be linked with Robert Lee, perhaps. . . . But she'd never make it if she allowed herself to be buddy-buddy with someone like Elena.

Lauralee's former resolve returned. She owed it to Mother and Dad, didn't she, to be a social success like Max? Being asked to that dance by Robert Lee was a priceless boon she could not lightly toss aside. She cast about for a way of escape. Let Elena solve her own problems.

"But what boy would ask me?" Elena's plaint seemed remote and far away. "With my out-of-fashion clothes and, what you call it, hair style that Father will not let me change, any boy would be ashamed to be seen."

Surprise jolted Lauralee. Elena was aware of her shortcomings? It was the first inkling she had of that. Certainly such an awareness was necessary before the shortcomings could be overcome, and it would have been painful to point them out to her.

Even so, what could she do to help her? Lauralee thought.

Her mind flitted back to her own pleasant situation. So nice a boy, Elena had called Robert Lee. It made her feel good to have even Elena say it. She should say something nice to Elena, too, something soothing and reassuring. But she could think of nothing except, "Oh, I wouldn't say that," and knew how inane and insincere it sounded.

Lauralee could never gush and mouth compliments she did not mean; only when she thought and felt something deeply could she put it into words.

Vainly she cast about for something polite and honest to say. But she could not think of a single thing.

They walked on in silence. Lauralee was glad it was only a short distance to the weather-beaten house beside the tracks. She had never felt so tongue-tied in her life.

She tried to recapture her own former pleasant state of mind. But somehow all she could think of was how glad she would be when she and Elena parted company at the walk leading to the Sloshek home.

"Won't you come in, please?" Elena asked when they reached it.

Lauralee's brave resolve melted like wax in a hot sun. "Just a moment," she faltered. "You see, my mother. . . ."

She was already going up the wooden steps and walking across the old-fashioned porch that stretched along the front of the ancient square house. Elena opened the door with the stiffly starched curtains framing its glass window.

Warily, as though guilty of wrong-doing, Lauralee glanced back at the walk and up and down the street. Was anyone she knew watching?

She stepped into the hallway. Whatever it was that she had expected, this wasn't it. Her first impression was one of whiteness, stiffly starched and immaculate, permeated with a delectable aroma of spicy sweetness.

A beaming, motherly figure appeared in a doorway at the rear of the hall. It was Mrs. Sloshek, a smile wreathing her rosy face, looking exactly like one of the Old World porcelain figures that Lauralee's mother kept in a glass-enclosed cabinet at home.

"Ah, mine Elena." Her voice overflowed with affection for her daughter and, at the same time, she took in with approval the stranger with her. Then she lapsed into a fluid flow of words, none of which Lauralee understood.

Feeling as if she had stepped into an illustration of a delicately-told folk tale of some enchanting land, Lauralee looked about. Design and color were everywhere—yet so combined with whiteness as to give a feeling of airy spaciousness. Home! Never had she seen it so exemplified as here.

Through an open doorway she saw a huge, round table, obviously for dining. It was covered with a cloth around the edge of which tiny Old World figures of boys and girls danced in a field of flowers. The bold, bright design was worked with intricate cross-stitch and a fringe, soft and full and a foot wide, hung almost to the floor. Mother would have swooned over it.

The café-like curtains were embroidered, too, in like designs, and the seats of the chairs were covered with embroidered cushions. In one corner stood a tall, old-fashioned press entirely covered with a lovely flowing pattern of hand-painted birds and flowers. A window chest was similarly decorated, as was a border around the calcimined walls.

"Mamma asks, will you stay for a cup of chocolate and some cakes?" Elena broke into her reverie, adding a bit shamefacedly, "Our home is old countryish, but please excuse."

Lauralee turned to face Elena. Somehow in these surroundings the dark, gypsylike girl looked almost beautiful.

"It's lovely!" she exclaimed, and never in her whole life had she made a more sincere statement.

Beaming, Mamma Sloshek led the way into the kitchen. Here, too, color and design were everywhere—on Mamma's apron, the snowy cloth on the kitchen table, the curtains, all embroidered. Lovely bird and flower motifs adorned cabinet doors, chair backs, flower pots holding red geraniums, and even the tin hood over the stove.

Lauralee was enchanted. "Did you do all this yourself?" she asked.

Elena nodded vigorously. "Mamma and I did." She laughed. "We Moravians cannot see a plain surface that we must paint or embroider a design on it."

Mrs. Sloshek set cups of steaming chocolate on the table, with generous blobs of whipped cream floating on top. She put out tiny plates and a large one in the center full of finger-sized cakes set in a bed of fluffy powdered sugar.

"Kipferdln," Mrs. Sloshek smiled as Lauralee took one of the powdery cakes.

Lauralee took a tiny bite from the end and the creamy deliciousness melted in her mouth. Such cakes had never come from a box of cake mix!

"Delicious," she said, and she meant that, too. She must get the recipe for those; the taste of them would send Dad into raptures for a week! "So is the chocolate. But they are sort of Austrian-ish, aren't they?" If her memory served her correctly one of her ancestors had emigrated from Austria.

Elena nodded. "Moravia was once a part of Austria-Hungary," she said. "It is now a province of Czechoslovakia."

Even Lauralee knew why many people had fled that unhappy land. Her heart went out to the Slosheks.

Though Mamma Sloshek spoke very broken English, she and Lauralee got along fine. Lauralee liked Elena better by the minute. She hated to leave but she had to go. Mother was attending a P.T.A. meeting at Binky's school and she had to start dinner. She got the recipe for *kipferdln* before she left.

"And remember," Mamma said, "a vanilla bean must be in the canister of powdered sugar!"

Lauralee nodded. She knew how such little things could add to the unique flavor of different foods.

"Do come again," Elena said eagerly as she bade Lauralee good-bye at the door.

"I will," Lauralee replied, "and you must come to see me."

Out on the porch she wondered why she had said that. Tomorrow the enchantment of Elena's surroundings would be gone; at school she would be the same funny foreigner.

She went down the steps. Then across the street she saw three girls walking along and looking straight at her. They were Eloise, Eileen and Marion. Her chances of ever becoming a part of their charmed circle had dimmed considerably.

Lauralee returned to present reality with a bang. For a brief time inside Elena's home she had forgotten all about the charmed circle. Now its importance loomed as great as ever. Would a friend of Elena's ever make it?

7

Big Night

Lauralee worried about it all through dinner. She stopped, though, when Mother mentioned the fact that the high school P.T.A. was holding a Bake Sale in the lobby of the Elm Park National Bank a week from today, and she was in charge of calling for donations.

That brought back sharp memories of Mrs. Sloshek's *kipferdln*. She told Mother about them. "They are delicious!" she cried, her mouth fairly watering at the thought of the creamy lusciousness of the finger-sized sweets. She went on then to tell about stopping at Elena's house and what an enchanting place it was, inside.

Mother was pleased. "I'll call Mrs. Sloshek," she said, "and ask her if she will make some for our Bake Sale."

Then Lauralee showed her the recipe Mrs. Sloshek had given her. Mrs. Larkin poured over it and shook her smartly coiffed head. "I would never be able to take the time to go through all this for the sake of some cookies."

Lauralee rolled her eyes and ran her tongue discreetly over her lips. "You would, Mother, if you had ever eaten any," she said.

"Perhaps," said Mother doubtfully. "But if I did, how could I ever make all the dresses and blouses and skirts I do for you and Maxine?"

That jolted Lauralee a bit, for she had been resenting, secretly, the chocolate pie Mother had made that morning and stored in the refrigerator for the evening meal. Its crushed vanilla-wafer crust needed no baking, and it was filled with instant pudding from a box and garnished with whipped cream. She couldn't imagine Mrs. Sloshek putting anything like that on the table for her loved ones.

But she guessed now that even mothers couldn't do *everything*. While Mother used short cuts in her baking she probably used the time saved to make the pretty clothes that she and Max were so proud to wear. While Mrs. Sloshek could and did bake delicious things to eat she certainly did not sew much—or stylishly anyhow.

Dad broke into her train of thought. "And what's the matter with an able-bodied girl of fourteen, who can read, making some of those kippered herring, or what-have-you?" he asked, wrinkling his nose so his glasses slid back into their proper place on its bridge.

"*Kippered herring!* Oh, Father!" Maxine dissolved into giggles.

"I'll make some tomorrow afternoon," Lauralee promised, tucking the recipe into her blouse pocket. She might not be as efficient as Max at straightening her room in the morning but she could cook better. Max, she thought with satisfaction, couldn't boil water without burning it!

Binky let out a groan. "I'll see if I can't get Grandma Coran to ask me over to her house for supper tomorrow," he said with exaggerated martyrdom.

Lauralee made a face at him. "Suit yourself," she said lightly. "Nothing you can say will keep me from trying." She meant it, too. She'd try to repay in a small way all the time Mother had spent on that velveteen dress.

She rose from the table, full of good intentions about helping Mother more, cleared away the dishes and rinsed them and stacked them in the dishwasher. Then she set the dials, and while it roared and churned she started up to her room.

As she passed through the hall Mother was just rising from what Dad called the gossip bench on which rested the downstairs telephone. Mrs. Larkin smiled fondly at Lauralee and said, "I've just talked to Mrs. Sloshek. She's promised to bake some *kipferdln*, as well as some other cookies for our Bake Sale. Thanks to you, Lee, perhaps we can get her to take a more active part in P.T.A. I don't believe anyone really tried to draw her in before."

"I'm so glad, Mother," Lauralee answered, pleased with herself. She went up the stairs fairly glowing in the knowledge that she had really done a good deed that day, even though unwillingly.

Then, a few minutes later, the glow subsided as her thoughts took another turn. Elena would think that Mrs. Larkin's call was directly linked with her visit that afternoon, which it was. She would get the idea from it that at last she had made a friend, one with whom she could talk in the corridors and walk home every afternoon.

"Oh, no," thought Lauralee, "I can't do that!" Oh, why hadn't she turned back that afternoon and gone home the other way? She wouldn't have seen the quaint and lovely interior of the Sloshek home or eaten the delicious *kipferdln,* but what she hadn't seen or tasted she wouldn't miss.

Goop stood forlornly in the center of her bed. In her preoccupation of the last few days she had neglected the stuffed giraffe. She picked him up now and hugged him. Left over from her toddler days, he had brought her many hours of comfort. He brought her *none* now.

Before her mind's eye passed the vision of Eloise and Eileen and Marion looking her way as she emerged from the Sloshek house. Had they recognized her? Of course they had. What had they thought and said? They would pass her up without a nod the next time they saw her; she was certain of that. Oh, if only she had Jenny again!

Jenny! Goop went flying and landed in a very undignified position at the foot of her bed.

"Where is my letter?" she cried looking around. It wasn't on her dresser or her nightstand. It wasn't on her desk. Come to think of it she hadn't brought one up that afternoon.

Out the door and down the stairs she flew. She looked on the table in the hall where Mother always left the day's mail for each recipient to pick up as he or she went by. There was no letter of any kind on that table.

"Mother!" she called, hearing footsteps in the kitchen followed by the slam of the refrigerator door. "Where is my letter?"

Binky popped his face through the kitchen door, stuffing a sandwich into his mouth—right after dinner, too.

"Letter?" His voice was muffled. "What letter?"

"My letter from Jenny!" wailed Lauralee.

"There was no letter from Jenny today," Mother's voice came from the living room. She, too, looked into the hall. Seeing the stricken look on her daughter's face, she added soothingly, "Perhaps it was a day late in delivery."

"Jenny didn't write!" Lauralee cried in a voice of anguish. She turned and fled up the stairs.

Once upstairs, after a few tears, she realized she had to pull herself together. She had homework, lots of it, to do. Listlessly, she settled Goop on her desk and began to work on her algebra assignment. By the time she turned off her light for the night she was resigned to life as it was and not as it ought to be.

Next morning things happened as she had expected. Eloise passed her in the hall, pert little nose in the air, acting as though she had never seen Lauralee before. They were so close that their skirts swished together, so Lauralee knew it was not a matter of the redhead not seeing or recognizing her. And Eileen and Marion did the same thing.

Elena greeted her with a warm smile and a shy "Good morning," and walked down the hall with her. Elena's eagerness to be friendly would have melted a heart of stone, and Lauralee's wasn't that. In a sudden spurt of good will she told Elena how she was going to make some *kipferdln* for her father that very afternoon. And Elena's eyes fairly shone with pleasure.

Lauralee's budding independence took on a slightly defiant tone. Why must she live in fear of what Eloise and her pals thought? She had a date with Robert Lee, didn't she? And *he* had seen her talking to Elena. He stopped and talked to her several times that day, and was especially attentive when Eloise was within seeing and hearing distance.

Once, when they were walking down a corridor talking and laughing, Eloise swished past. "I hope you have a *marvelous* time at the dance Saturday night," she smirked. And the way she said it her meaning could have been interpreted several ways.

Puzzled, Lauralee looked after her. Had that remark been made out of jealousy? Was that, after all, the reason for the snub of the morning? Laughter bubbled up inside Lauralee. This was rich.

Robert Lee watched Eloise, too. He shook his head and said, "Tsk, tsk! Ah always heard redheads had terrible tempers. Now Ah know it."

Lauralee wondered then just how Robert Lee really felt about Eloise. Of course, she knew she hadn't been his first choice as a date. But after Eloise he had chosen her and that was some comfort.

Actually she found it a relief to throw off such cares and bake the *kipferdln* when she got home that afternoon. While they didn't taste quite as delicious as Mrs. Sloshek's, they were pretty good for a first attempt. Dad, of course, ate several and said they were positively scrumptious.

Friday afternoon Robert Lee stopped her on the school steps and told her again what time he would come for her Saturday evening.

"Mother will drive us," he said, looking embarrassed. With a deep sigh, he added, "Ah shuah will be mighty happy when Ah have a driver's license and can drive all by mahself."

Lauralee nodded happily though sympathetically. This business of having parents drive couples to the dance seemed an almost unbearable disgrace to the boys, though it mattered little to their dates. All the boys gave the impression they were living only for their junior year when they could take the Driver Training course and get their licenses to pilot the family cars. Boys were funny that way. They wanted so much to grow up quickly and become independent.

Eloise passed them then and, with a pert flip of her head at Robert Lee, went down the steps and started walking home with Bud.

The next day, Saturday, was a busy one. At least a half dozen times Lauralee tried on the velveteen dress, thankful that it zippered up much of the way so that she didn't disturb all the rollers and pincurls Maxine had put in her hair.

"You'd think she was a queen getting ready for her coronation," Dad grinned as he went about his Saturday chores.

"It probably seems that important to her," Mother replied.

Maxine was much more helpful than Lauralee thought she would be, brushing and combing her hair as carefully as she did her own.

"Now, don't try to play the *femme fatale* bit," she admonished sternly. "You weren't cut out for it."

Lauralee whirled. "Now what did you mean by that?" she demanded, remembering all too well the fluttering of Max's lashes and the coy toss of the blond bob when her sister wanted to put across a point with Wayne or Tiny. "You mean I'm not the flirty type?"

"That is exactly what I mean," Max replied bluntly. "Reserved is what you should be, though not so much so you become a bore."

"Well, thank you Miss-Adviser-to-the-Lovelorn," Lauralee snapped and took the comb away from Max and defiantly brought down a wisp of bang. Wasn't it bad enough to have Mother and Dad hint that Maxine was more their idea of the ideal daughter? Did Maxine herself have to act so insufferably superior?

"Well, nobody is so perfect she can't benefit by some well-meant advice," Max shot back.

Lauralee knew that was so, though she wouldn't have admitted it to anyone. With each passing minute she was becoming more jittery and unsure of herself. Her first real date! With a boy she didn't really know very well. If it were Bud—well, she wouldn't have to wonder how to act around him.

She thought of all sorts of quips and witty things to say. Boys liked to talk about themselves. Well, she would talk only about Robert Lee, and what was it like in Birmingham, and sports, and such things as that. She'd be very casual about it, too, as though dating was an everyday experience for her.

She worried about her dancing. She hadn't tried very hard to learn at the junior high dancing classes. She hadn't been interested then. Would she get her feet all tangled up on the floor? Her chin went up as she twirled about before her full-length mirror. Of course, she wouldn't. She'd be as graceful as a gazelle. Graceful! With her big feet?

She alternated between bliss and despair. When dinner

time came she was so nervous she only picked at her food.

Ten minutes before Robert Lee was due she pirouetted before her mirror for the umpteenth time and her courage returned, full force. She looked quite nice if she did say so herself. Thanks to Maxine her hair was lovely, shining, lifted off her forehead and swept back in a series of gentle waves that ended in a large rolling curl at her shoulders. The richness of the color and texture of the velveteen dress gave her tanned skin a healthy glow and the flared skirt swayed gracefully as she moved. The picture of youthful good looks that smiled back at her was enhanced by a wee bit of lipstick and the shining strand of the tiny chain about her neck from which hung the heart-shaped locket, centered by a chip diamond, that Dad had given her for her birthday. Just old-fashioned enough to be modernly charming.

"Not bad," she thought, and childishly stuck out her tongue at her reflection. Picking up her fluffy white shortie coat and clutch bag, she started downstairs.

"Wow!" yelped Binky, skidding to a stop in the hall as he saw her coming sedately down the steps.

Dad could see her from the living room. He gave a low, admiring whistle and Mother beamed proudly.

"Lee!" Maxine's horrified voice came from the head of the stairs. "Come back up here and stay until your date comes!"

Lauralee looked back, puzzled. "Why? I'm ready."

"Well, for goodness' sake, don't let him *know* it!"

Lauralee's puzzlement grew. She looked at Binky, who shrugged and gazed cynically at the ceiling, saying in effect that such feminine foibles were far beyond his masculine comprehension. Lauralee hesitated.

Maxine raced down the stairs then and almost yanked Lauralee back up. "Boy, have you got a lot to learn!" she panted.

Then Lauralee remembered that Maxine never came downstairs until her date had cooled his heels in the hall or living room for at least five minutes.

Once inside the door of their room Maxine demanded, "Do you want him to get the idea you are looking forward to his coming?"

"Why not? I am, really."

Maxine shook her head despairingly. "Never let a boy know you are interested in him, even if you are."

"But the other night you said to let Bud know I wanted him to take me."

"Of course, but play it softly, child, softly."

Lauralee snorted. "Well, if you're so smart at this business why isn't Wayne taking you?" The minute the words were out she knew she shouldn't have said that. The hairbrush slowed in its downward movement through the blond tresses and Max's blue eyes stared at her from the mirror.

"I'm sorry," Lauralee said lamely.

Maxine's mouth went grim. "Well, I just wanted you to avoid making the same mistakes I have," she said softly.

Lauralee stared at the back of Maxine's head. Max had made mistakes? Who was she kidding?

The bell rang then. Mother's voice came up to them.

"Lauralee," she called.

Remembering again how Max would do it, Lauralee answered, "Be down in a minute, Mother."

Her heart raced and her mouth felt suddenly as though she had swallowed a spoonful of cornstarch. Robert Lee Morton was down there waiting for her, to take her to a dance. The wonder of it. But could she go down and face him? For a brief second she felt like calling the whole thing off.

Instead, she waited as Max would have done. Then she slowly made her grand entrance.

Robert Lee's eyes were frankly admiring as he watched her come down. Lauralee's confidence shot sky high. She was glad that Mother and Dad did not make a big thing of it. They just said casually, "Have a good time," and let her and Robert Lee go.

Once in the rear seat of the car Lauralee's self-confidence took wing and flew away. She could not think of a thing to say beyond, "How do you do, Mrs. Morton?"

In his mother's presence Robert Lee seemed to lose his suavity, too. He seemed much younger than at school and more, well, adolescent, Lauralee thought. Why she had thought he was so special she couldn't think right now.

Mrs. Morton chattered on, trying, it seemed, to fill the void of silence in the rear seat. She asked Lauralee all sorts of questions. Lauralee gave the shortest answers possible in a sort of hoarse whisper.

She could not think of a single one of the clever things she had planned to say.

Twice Robert Lee tried to shush his mother with an embarrassed "Oh, Ma!" Once was when she told of a funny happening—to her it was funny anyway—when Robert was three years old, and the other was when she told of his fear that it might be hard for a southern boy to make friends up north. Both Lauralee and Robert Lee were relieved when they slid out of the car in front of the school.

"Have a good tahm." Mrs. Morton smiled at them from the dimly lit recesses of the car. "And, Bobby, call when y'all are ready to go home."

Lauralee saw Robert Lee wince at the Bobby part, and she felt downright sorry for him. But then it seemed most teens had such trouble with their parents who found it difficult to realize that their little ones were growing up.

The minute the Morton car shot away, their grown-up feelings returned. Robert Lee was again the suave young gentleman, holding open the heavy school door as she slid through.

Lauralee's tongue loosened surprisingly and she began to chatter as they walked down the brightly lit corridor toward the cafeteria.

Other couples were drifting toward the scene of festivities. She and Robert Lee greeted some of them as though they had known them intimately for a long time.

With Robert Lee's hand lightly on her elbow Lauralee made for the hall closet where wraps were being checked. She handed over her white coat and Robert put the check into his coat pocket. Then they headed for the bright and festive-looking cafeteria.

The big night had begun.

8

A Different Person

Bud and Eloise were dancing to the music of Hester's Hot Shots all by themselves on the spotlighted floor. It was Eloise's idea to make themselves so conspicuous, Lauralee was certain of that. Why not? She was a knockout.

The burnished red-gold hair of Bud's date shone like a beacon above the short white tulle dancing frock with billowing skirt that swung gracefully about her slender legs. Fully aware of the dreamy picture she and tall, athletic Bud made, she was eager to play the role of belle of the ball to the very hilt.

One glance at Robert Lee showed her the impact had not been lost on him. His eyes followed every move Bud and Eloise made. When they passed by, his eyes were leveled at Eloise and she smiled back, in a special sort of way, that plainly said this was for one evening only. Everyone around took notice, but it didn't mean as much to them as it did to Lauralee.

While other couples began to take courage and drift onto the floor, Lauralee hung back reluctantly, her self-confidence and high hopes withered to almost nothing. The red dress, she was certain, hung limp on her tall, thin frame, feeling homemade and frumpy. Her legs were suddenly too long and awkward as sticks, her feet too big—and what should she do with her hands? Her hairdo felt ridiculous and she had a sudden urge to flee.

Nobody would miss her.

"The way she holds her head a body'd think she had a crick in her neck," a soft chuckle sounded in her ear. She whirled.

"Who?" she asked dazedly.

"Why, the duchess, who else?" Robert Lee nodded in Eloise's direction. How could he be so irreverent about a walking dream? But of course, he was saying that because the walking dream wasn't with *him*.

"Let's dance," he said, and slipping his arm about her waist, he guided her onto the slippery floor.

It was like keeping your balance on ice skates if you weren't a very good skater. Lauralee's feet, almost, but not quite, went out from under her. Robert Lee's hold tightened and kept her upright. Flustered she looked around. Had anyone noticed? Not Eloise or Bud, thank goodness. They were at the other end of the floor, moving their feet in one spot while they talked to Tom Harris and his date. But what did Robert Lee think of her?

Whatever his feelings he kept them to himself. With masterly ease, as though he were well accustomed to catching stumbling partners, he swept her around the floor, executing little steps she had not learned in her junior high dancing classes. She found she could follow him perfectly.

"Did anybody evah tell y'all what a fine dancah you are?"

he asked, a grin playing about his well-shaped mouth. And he said it without a trace of sarcasm. A pleased thrill went through Lauralee.

"Oh, sure," she laughed. She might as well act gay and festive even if she felt the opposite. "Lots and lots of boys."

With that blatant exaggeration her good humor did return. She simply was not going to allow that big oaf Bud and his date spoil this evening that she had looked forward to for so long.

Robert Lee had apparently made up his mind to the same thing. He tightened his arm about her waist and they danced around the floor. But Lauralee noticed he seemed to take delight in coming as close to Bud and Eloise as possible.

No wonder. He could dance circles around Bud, who sort of hip-hopped awkwardly around, one, two, three, dance-class fashion. She could almost see Bud's lips move in count to the beat of the music as he struggled around the floor.

"And I thought *I* looked awkward," she thought with a tinge of satisfaction. Actually she felt as light as a breeze and as graceful as a butterfly. Dancing was no effort for Robert Lee. He just breezed around, thoroughly enjoying himself—none of which was lost on Eloise who seemed downright chagrined at the close attention he was paying to Lauralee.

Lauralee was pleased now. Her returning self-confidence made her more critical of Eloise. Actually the redhead's hairdo was a trifle overdone and her frock was too frou-frou for chic. And the stark whiteness of the dress empha-sized the freckles and the somewhat large nose and bony features. Bud and Eloise looked much more romantic at a distance, she decided.

While she and Robert Lee were not so spectacular, she felt they were more attractive in a conservative sort of way. Her partner did not jitterbug, hop, or gyrate like some of the boys or use the one, two, three, slide, of others. His dancing was smooth, in perfect time to the music, and she followed each step with grace and precision.

Her new-found poise and confidence caused Lauralee to do things she wouldn't have dreamed of doing otherwise. She laughed rather loudly and conspicuously at every remark, no matter how inconsequential, that Robert Lee made, looking up at him and flapping her lashes as she did so. Especially when Bud and Eloise were near.

Bud noticed, of course, and grinned at her in that indulgent, boy-next-door sort of way. This gave Robert Lee the chance he had apparently been waiting for.

"How about switching pahtners, Bud?" he said jovially, trying to make his suggestion appear to be a big joke, just in case Bud turned him down. But Bud had no choice. Eloise had slipped from his arms and stepped over beside Robert Lee before he had an opportunity to express an opinion one way or the other. She took the southern boy's arm in a proprietary sort of way.

"I'd *love* to, honey," she said, and she gave him a heart-melting look. Her nose looked perfect then and there was nothing bony about her features. How could any boy resist her? Lauralee thought bitterly.

Robert Lee lost no time in whisking Eloise across the floor, leaving Bud and Lauralee becalmed in the sea of dancers whirling about them.

"Let's sit this one out," Bud said gruffly and anyone could see he was angry beyond words. He started to lead Lauralee off the floor and she had no choice but to follow him.

When they were halfway across the floor the voice of the orchestra leader, bellowing through a microphone, stopped them. "Now, we'll have the grand march. Bring your partners and line up at the left of the floor."

And unwilling partners though they were, Bud and Lauralee were swept into it willy-nilly and walked around the floor in that silly march—an endless number of times it seemed to her. Bud grew grumpier with each encirclement.

"Oh, boy! Big deal! Some fun!" he kept repeating over and over.

At every turn they saw the laughing faces of Eloise and Robert Lee. They were having a ball and it was easy to see they had no regrets at pairing off together.

Lauralee tried to cover her true feelings of frustrated confusion by waving and chatting with almost anyone near her, whether she knew them or not. And when Tom Harris or Leo Holt or Ben Thomas came near she flirted with them outrageously, even though Maxine's disapproving eyes were upon her several times and she knew it.

But Lauralee didn't care. She was going to show Bud and Robert Lee and anyone else who might be interested that she was fourteen and fancy-free and they could like it or not as they pleased. No old boy was going to make a ninny out of her!

But all the same she kept an eye on Robert Lee, looking

for a weakening in his obvious pleasure at being with Eloise.

He came back briefly. During one of the musicians' many intermissions he asked, "Would ya'll like a cup of punch?"

She lifted her chin proudly and answered coolly, "Bud has already gone for some." She waved her hand and, to prove her point, there came Bud across the floor, gingerly holding two small plates, with a paper cup of pink liquid and a cooky on each. Somebody bumped into him and he did some fancy juggling while good-natured laughs followed in his wake.

Robert Lee quickly took advantage of the situation. "Then Ah'll go get some for Eloise," he said almost gratefully, and was off like a shot.

Lauralee didn't have another chance to talk to him. An hour later Bud told her gloomily, "How do ya like that? That rebel and Eloise just left with a bunch of other guys and gals. Took off for the Pizza Palace. Said they'd be back in a little while."

He slid disgustedly into one of the folding chairs placed around the edge of the cafeteria. The crowd was getting thinner as couples drifted off the floor and down the hall toward the phone booths where they called home to ask someone to come and pick them up.

Lauralee was sick at heart. If this was one of the big date affairs she had heard so much about, the other girls could have them. She was thoroughly disenchanted and wished she had never come.

Then Mrs. Newton appeared in the doorway and waved, trying to get Bud's attention. "There's your mother," Lauralee hissed loudly, hoping he would hear.

Bud looked up. A look of pure relief swept across his face.

"Yeah, she said she'd stop by and pick us up after her committee meeting at the Youth Center." Mrs. Newton, too, was very active in parents' organizations at the school and served on various committees. Lauralee hadn't been to the Youth Center, which was about a block from the school and a favorite hangout for many freshmen as well as a few upperclassmen, and right now she was certain she never wanted to go.

Bud turned to Lauralee. "Ready to go?" he asked, as though she were a flea or something.

Lauralee shrugged. She didn't have to pretend for Bud either. "Why not?" she answered.

Robert Lee had the check for her white coat. But she knew Mrs. Adams, one of the P.T.A. members helping out at the checking concession for the evening.

She got her coat and Bud left the check for Eloise's wrap. "Serve her right if she never got it," he said grimly.

"Let's not be bitter," Lauralee said brightly, thinking it was the only sensible thing she had said all evening.

When Mrs. Newton saw Bud emerge from the school with Lauralee she looked surprised. She had driven Bud and Eloise *to* the dance. But she shrugged the matter off as if to say one could never tell what teens were apt to do. This was her third child to guide through the teen years and she had apparently long ago decided not to let such things bother her.

The ride home was silent and grim.

"Oh, I hope Mom and Dad aren't waiting up for me." Opening the door of her home Lauralee shut her eyes and breathed deeply. She certainly didn't want to answer any of their probing questions tonight.

She slipped into the hallway as quietly as she could, up the stairs and into her room and then out of her clothes and into bed. Some minutes later she heard the door open but she lay still trying to give the impression that she was exhausted from all the fun she had had and just wanted to rest.

Mother took the hint and gently closed the door and left.

A tear squeezed from Lauralee's eyes onto the pillow, and then another. How could an evening promise to be such a joy and turn into such a nightmare? Clutching Goop she hugged him, as she had on so many troubled occasions. She dropped off to sleep so quickly she did not even hear Max come in.

The minute she opened her eyes next morning Maxine demanded, "Who came home with you last night anyway?"

"Bud. Why?"

"Well, Robert Lee was looking all over for you."

Lauralee sat up in bed, hair tousled and eyes flashing.

"Oh, he was, was he? Well, what do you know?"

Had he thought she would stand around waiting for him after he had gone off with Eloise? Boys, for all she cared, could go fly their kites. From this day on she wasn't going to be interested in any of them. She flopped back on her bed, covered her head with the sheet, and lay there, seething.

9

Competition

Monday morning, as she stepped off the bus, Robert Lee came toward her.

"Lauralee, Ah, uh . . ." he stammered, red-faced.

"Good morning, *Bobby,*" she replied icily, "how are *y'all?*"

Several times during the day he tried to talk to her but she avoided him.

In each class she was a perfect student, missing nothing, taking notes, studying, concentrating. She made it a point to walk down the corridor with Elena, discussing the next day's Latin assignment. She went out of her way to be friendly with Annie David, too. Annie showed her a poster she was making for the P.T.A. Bake Sale and they talked of the rewards of creative work.

"I'd rather draw than eat," Annie said and, while Lauralee thought that was taking it a bit too far, she was sympathetic.

That was the sort of thing, she vowed, she was going to be interested in from now on, something worthwhile, something besides boys and clothes, clothes and boys. She couldn't draw, but there were other things. When she left school that afternoon she fairly staggered under the weight of the books she carried.

She had just settled down at her desk and started work on her social studies assignment when Mother called from downstairs, "Lauralee, Robert Lee Morton is on the phone."

Disgustedly she threw down her pencil. Couldn't he take a hint? Weren't there enough boy-crazy girls at school so he didn't have to keep bothering her?

"Tell him, I. . . ." Well, she couldn't say she didn't want to talk to him; her mother would think that very rude. "I'll take it up here," she called back.

Going into the upstairs hall she picked up the receiver and breathed a blithe "Hi," into the mouthpiece. She'd be cool and distant so he wouldn't get the idea she was going into a decline over him.

"Ah just wanted to say again how sorry Ah am about last Saturday ev'nin'," Robert Lee said hastily as though afraid she might hang up on him before he was through. "We just stepped out to the Pizza Palace and came right back and— y'all were gone. Ah was mortified."

"Ooooh, think nothing of it. I had another escort home."

Was that a sigh of relief she heard? Had he apologized only because his mother had made him? He wasn't really sorry, she was certain, that he had traded her company for that of Eloise. Only Bud was. But not for anything would she let him suspect that she cared one way or the other.

She chatted with him for a moment, nothing personal. Then she went back to her studies. But first she reread for the umpteenth time a letter she had received that day from Jenny.

"I'll never get used to it out here," Jenny wailed on paper. "Not in a hundred years. How I wish I were back in Elm Park."

It was such a comfort to learn her friend was unhappy, too!

Lauralee's dedicated program went on for several days. Mother began to look a bit anxious.

"Now, don't overdo it, dear," Mrs. Larkin said one afternoon as Lauralee went straight to her room to begin studying. "Remember, all work and no play—"

"Don't worry, Mother. I know what I'm doing," Lauralee answered lightly and kept on going.

To tell the truth, though, she was beginning to feel the need to let up a little. So instead of studying until dinner time that evening she washed her hair and experimented with a new way of putting it up on rollers.

"Boy, you look like a sick porcupine," Binky remarked when she came down with her hair still up.

"Use my little dryer, Lee," Mother said tactfully. "It will be a half hour before dinner is ready."

So she went back upstairs and dug out the dryer. When she came down again her hair was dry and combed and looked nice; Dad said so.

That evening she answered a letter from Jenny.

"There's a boy next door who isn't so bad," Jenny had written. "I talk to him some."

Lauralee wasn't as scornful of her friend's defection as she might have been a few days ago. She and Robert Lee were again on speaking terms and she had decided that perhaps boys weren't so bad, in small doses.

She went downstairs to join Maxine and the other seniors, who had gathered to ready the recreation room for the party at which the exchange students, Jennie Matsuko and Mary Kelly, were to be the guests of honor.

They planned to give the room a Japanese-Irish atmosphere and, as Binky said, it wasn't easy.

Such hustle and bustle, everybody getting in everybody else's way. Lauralee found it fun, though, to work with so large a group and she was surprised how hard Maxine worked. Her sister was here and there and everywhere while tiny paper Japanese lanterns were hung from the ceiling, mingled with green and white streamers. Gilded cardboard dragons marched around the walls, with green shamrocks in between. A wide piece of plywood was laid across the Ping-pong table and covered with a green cloth.

"Looks great," they all agreed when the job was finished and they sat around drinking Cokes. "It takes Maxine to dream up nice parties."

Maxine beamed, and both Wayne and Tiny drank a toast to that. Lauralee, sitting on the stairway with Binky, realized for the first time that Maxine had always been a tireless giver of parties. Was that the reason for some of her popularity?

She thought about it again the next evening when a large group of seniors gathered in the softly lit recreation room for the party. Maxine was here and there all evening, seeing to it that everybody had a good time. She led the games and group singing and, when things seemed to drag a little, put records on the record player that set couples dancing.

The exchange students were an instant hit.

The girls from Japan and Ireland seemed pleased by the American-style party and, quickly catching the spirit of it, enjoyed themselves thoroughly.

"What a nice party!" everybody said upon leaving.

"I'm exhausted," Maxine murmured as she fell into bed that night. Maxine deserved to be treated as a social queen for a few days, Lauralee thought then. Perhaps she should find something like that to busy herself with. But what?

Monday afternoon, in homeroom, it was announced that the freshman classes would hold an election two weeks from that date. They would select their class president, vice-president, secretary, and treasurer.

"Anyone can run for the office of his choice," the announcement ran, "after turning in a petition, signed by twenty-five of his classmates, to the president of the student council. He or she may run independently or on a party ticket with running mates. Each office will be filled by the candidate receiving the most votes."

As the announcement was read an idea formed quickly in Lauralee's mind. What better way of distinguishing herself than becoming a class officer? All the way home she thought about it. Once upstairs, with her homework spread out on her desk, she gazed out the window and concentrated on it even more. Should she? Shouldn't she?

Voices drifted up from the yard below. Soon Binky's voice bellowed, "Where's Dad's monkey wrench?"

"With his tools, of course," she shouted back.

"I can't find it."

"You can't find anything," she said in annoyance, "unless it jumps right up and bites you. Who wants it?"

"Bud needs it."

Lauralee sighed. Her first inclination was to let Bud solve his own problems. Then an idea came to her. She got up and started down the stairs and then on to the basement. In a utility room by the furnace, on a shelf with Mr. Larkin's tools, lay the wrench, in plain sight.

"Was this what you wanted, Binky?" She picked it up and held it under her small brother's nose.

"Well, it wasn't there when *I* looked," he blustered.

"I know. It just gets up and moves around by itself every once in a while."

"Very funny."

Together they went upstairs again and out the kitchen door where Bud waited. "Sorry I caused you so much trouble." He grinned.

"Oh, no trouble at all," Lauralee answered airily. Then she dropped her blockbuster. "I've decided to run for class president."

Bud's thick brows went up. "You don't say!" he cried. "Well, you'll have some stiff competition."

"Who?" she asked saucily. Eloise, she had just learned, was dating Robert Lee again. What did Bud think of that? Would he ever douse the torch he carried for that little flirt? Not that she cared—of course not!

But she had to admit that she felt differently about him now than she had even a few weeks before. He wasn't, well, just the boy next door now, but a rather attractive member of the opposite sex!

Bud looked down at her. Was his attitude toward her changing a bit, too?

"Who is going to be your competition?" he asked, grinning widely. "Me!" He turned to leave.

"I'll risk it," she said more lightly than she felt and went back into the house.

She began mapping her campaign at once. She decided not to run as an independent, rather, she would try to persuade three others to run for the other offices and so form a party.

She would call it the Popular Party.

Her enthusiasm rose. Campaign ideas began running through her head. Hard work? Of course it would be hard work. But if Max wasn't afraid of it, neither was she.

First things first. She'd start getting those twenty-five names the very first thing in the morning.

She was ten minutes early at the bus stop. Tammy and Susan shrugged and signed. They weren't obligated to vote for her in the election so it didn't matter to them. They were friendlier to her than they had been, but they still stuck together just as she and Jenny had.

Jenny! There had been no letter from Jenny yesterday. And that was the third time that had happened.

"We'll write to each other every day until we're both old ladies," they had promised each other when Jenny had moved. Now, less than two months later Jenny was slipping up on her promise. Was it because of that boy next door that she had written about? Oh, no! Not Jenny, in whose life boys meant less than nothing.

Lauralee happened to remember then that she had been

so busy last evening thinking of running for class president that she hadn't written to Jenny either. This afternoon she would write, the minute she got home.

Bud sat down beside her on the bus. He pulled out a sheet of paper with at least a dozen names on it.

"If you'll sign mine I'll sign yours," he said with a chuckle. "So long as we're rivals we might as well be friendly ones, eh?"

"Why, certainly," replied Lauralee, feeling a rising tide of pleasure at having Bud beside her. Of course, he was there only to get her name on his petition. She took her ball-point pen from a notebook and signed. He did the same on her sheet, blank except for the names of Tammy and Susan. She'd have to hustle to catch up with him.

"Thanks," Bud said and got up and went to the rear, pausing for another signature on the way. He had *more* friends!

Lauralee sat alone on the way to school, just as she did every morning. All the others were paired off or in groups. This aloneness would cost her a lot of votes unless she did something about it, and quick.

Should she run at all? She began to wonder. Of course she would; she had known when she decided to do so that it wouldn't be easy.

Elena Sloshek stood beside the steps of the school. Lauralee went up to her and greeted her warmly and told her of her desire to run for president. Would she sign her petition?

"Happy I am to sign," Elena replied, adding, "You will make a good class officer."

"Oh, thank you," said Lauralee feeling much better.

She had one friend anyhow—besides Jenny, of course.

Elena caught sight of another girl she knew, Hazel Walsh, and asked her to sign for Lauralee. Hazel did, timidly.

Lauralee knew Hazel only by name but decided right then and there she would try to get better acquainted with this shy, retiring girl. While the three girls stood talking, Hazel indicated another girl going up the steps.

"I'll ask Mildred to sign for you." And she did.

"Mildred Miller, what a pretty name," Lauralee said and Mildred smiled, pleased. She was a very plain girl and seemed painfully aware of it.

This was the way to do it, Lauralee thought with satisfaction—be friendly and outgoing with everybody. She smiled so much that morning that her jaws ached, but by noon she had the required number of names on her petition. With a feeling of real accomplishment she handed it to the freshman representative of the Student Council.

Now she would have to form a party, ask others to run for the other offices on her ticket. Boldly she decided to ask some of the most popular boys and girls in her class to run with her.

She went right up to Eloise Fisher and asked her to run for vice-president on the Popular Party slate. Eloise was friendly, or at least she wasn't unfriendly. But her no was firm.

"I'm not going to run for any class office," she said with a saucy toss of her red-gold hair, "until I am a senior. Then I shall run for *president*." She gave Lauralee a slightly patronizing look as she added, "Being an officer in your *senior* year is *much* more *important* than any other time."

Lauralee gulped. Then she remembered to be friendly and outgoing so she smiled and replied, "Well, *vote* for me, Eloise, will you?"

Eloise dimpled. "Oh, *dahling,*" she cried, "how can I promise that before I know who else is running?"

They parted on good terms though. Lauralee comforted herself with the thought that, if she hadn't snared a vote, she hadn't lost one for sure either.

Jim Talbot she knew only by name, but she did know he was tall, blond, lean, and very popular. She used her best wiles on him.

"I hadn't planned on running for any office," he grinned good-naturedly. "But seeing it's for you, I'll run for veep on your ticket."

"Oh, joy!" cried Lauralee. He would be a real asset as a running mate.

Now, who else? She decided to ask Annie David to run for secretary. Annie wasn't exactly popular, but she could make the loveliest posters, and they would need a lot of them. Annie seemed pleased to accept.

"Ah'm sorry, Lauralee," Robert Lee Morton said politely, "but Ah'm committed to another ticket." So were several others she asked.

So she wound up asking Elena to run for treasurer. The foreign-born girl wasn't within striking distance of the charmed circle but it might be that others in her circumstances would vote for her for that very reason. Elena was pleased to accept, too.

The Popular Party held their first meeting in the recreation room of the Larkin home. They discussed their platform and the coming campaign. Lauralee had some very definite ideas about the campaign.

"This must be run seriously," she said firmly. "Nothing silly."

"No stunts?" asked Jim.

Lauralee shook her head. "Just speeches," she said, "telling what we will do when elected, how hard we will work for the good of all, and that sort of thing."

"Yaaaay!" yelled Binky from the steps. He was promptly ordered out by his irate sister.

Annie agreed to design posters, campaign buttons, and streamers, and the others agreed to help make them. A slogan, "Hop to the Top With the Popular Party," was unanimously accepted.

The meeting lasted for an hour. By the time they were ready for refreshments Lauralee was as pleased as could be with the way things had gone.

"We'll win," she said confidently.

After the others had left, Binky returned. "Convention over?" he asked, looking mockingly solemn.

"Yes, and after you left we got a lot of things done," Lauralee said pointedly.

"Izzat so? Well, I'll have you know I went to another meeting, at Bud's, and I didn't get thrown out of it." He picked up a Coke bottle to help her clear things away. "Come to think of it, they didn't do anything but goof off."

Lauralee sort of smirked at that. Was that the stiff competition Bud had spoken of?

10

Going Her Way!

All through the busy days of the campaign Lauralee's hopes rose to great heights, then dropped abruptly to new lows. One day she was certain the Popular Party would win—by a small margin, perhaps, but it would win. The next day she was equally certain that it would be defeated. It was going to be a very close election; they were going to win by a landslide; they were going down to ignominious defeat.

Her hopes of victory rose to a new high, though, when she learned the name of the party Bud was heading.

"We're the Mavericks," he grinned when she asked him. "Just a herd of lost and unbranded critters! Yippee!" His shout ripped through the bus and caused riders and driver to turn to see what catastrophe had overtaken the ones in the rear. Bud had a voice like a foghorn and even when he whispered it could be heard across a room.

Lauralee smiled to herself rather smugly. If such non-sense was going to characterize the whole campaign of Bud's silly party, then it wouldn't be any competition at all. He and his running mates were going about the thing all wrong. Election of class officers was a serious business and should be conducted as such. Her classmates would be offended if it were made into a three-ring circus.

They wouldn't elect a clown for a president!

She couldn't write off the other two parties so lightly. One was called the Experts and the other was called the Astronauts—two very good names with lots of possibilities, the Astronauts, especially. Why hadn't she thought of that name first? It sounded so progressive and forward thinking, while Popular Party had an ordinary ring to it. Oh, well, it was too late now to change that.

As quietly as she could she tried to find out something about the slates and kinds of campaigns the Experts and Astronauts were planning to wage. To her utter dismay she learned that Sam Tabor was heading the Expert ticket. Though she didn't know Sam to speak to him she knew all about him, that he was a formidable scholar, an outstanding athlete, and one of the most all-around, popular students to come from Salt Creek Junior High. He would have many loyal followers.

To make things worse for the Popular Party, Robert Lee Morton was running for veep on his ticket. That southern drawl would gather in votes by the buckets!

As for the Astronauts—well, that name would be hard to beat. Susan Harris was running for president on that ticket, and she was as clever as they come and onstage so much, figuratively speaking, being a cheerleader at all the games. And Dave Foxe, well, with his guitar and softly sung folk songs he was a sparkler at any gathering.

It would take some doing to win this election. Lauralee

began to work hard on her speech.

"Fellow classmates," it began in a very serious tone, "I stand before you today asking that you elect me president of our class for this, our freshman year."

That, she felt, had the proper ring of dignity.

"Naturally," it went on, "you want to know the kind of person for whom you are asked to vote for this high office. So I will tell you of some of what I consider my more worthy accomplishments." As proof of her integrity and leadership she went on to list all past responsible positions she had held —treasurer of the sixth grade at Willard School, secretary of her Sunday School class two years before, and the leading roles she had taken in her Girl Scout group. She elaborated on each one as much as she could.

"Gee!" Binky cried with exaggerated admiration from the basement steps where, unknown to her, he had been listening to her run through her speech. "You sound like you had just stepped out of *Who's Who.*"

Lauralee whirled, her face scarlet. "Mother!" she wailed in anguish. "Make him get out of here!"

Mother's voice, gently chiding, came from upstairs. "Binky!"

"I'm leaving!" Binky chortled obligingly as he rose and clattered back up toward the kitchen. "Boy, I couldn't stand any more of *that!*"

Exasperated beyond words Lauralee ran her fingers through her thick hair. *Nobody* at home, it seemed, was interested in cooperating with her at all. So what was the use? She rolled up her speech and stalked upstairs and pitched it into a drawer of her desk. She'd simply forget the whole thing, she decided.

An hour later she took it out and read it through again, this time silently. You could never tell when that sneaky Binky was lurking about. It did need some polishing, she decided, so she added a word here and took away one there and changed a whole sentence in another place.

Then she arose and carefully locked the door of her room, for she knew Max wasn't coming until late that afternoon. With attention to gestures and voice inflection this time, she began reading it through aloud again. When she came to the part where she had been so rudely interrupted by Binky, she was especially dramatic for this, she felt, was most important. It told her classmates what she would work for, if elected. Better relations with parents and teachers was one thing that would receive her close attention, she vowed, as well as better cooperation with the Student Council and a really bang-up participation in Homecoming. When the last word rolled off her tongue a feeling of complete satisfaction with her efforts, and a conviction of victory, swept over her. She sat down on the edge of her bed, picked up Goop and hugged him ecstatically.

Then her gaze fell on two letters from Jenny that had lain, unopened, on her desk for—how long? Oh, dear, she'd have to read them, she supposed, and answer them this very evening or Jenny's feelings would be hurt. She couldn't do that to one who had been such a good friend, even if it had been ages ago.

Opening one of the letters—she might as well do it now and get it over with—she read with growing dismay that Jenny no longer had anything to do with the boy next door—he was dating another girl anyway. Wanda, the girl she had thought was sort of a friend, was the usurper and now she had no further use for her either. Jenny's letter was page after page of misery and how she wished she were back in Elm Park.

Lauralee sighed as she laid the pages down. She should feel more sympathy for Jenny, she supposed. But the trouble with Jenny really was that she wasn't doing anything worthwhile, like running for president of her class. If she were, she would be busy and happy like—well—like Lauralee. A girl simply could not sit still and expect life to come to her; she had to be outgoing and meet it, instead.

Her own letter to Jenny was four pages long. Into it she poured all her cheer, hoping to help Jenny see the errors of her ways. Very subtly she suggested that Jenny do as she was doing, that it would make their separation easier for both to bear.

Next day she and Annie and Jim and Elena met at Jim's home. They read their speeches to each other and listened to suggestions for making them better, both in context and delivery. Lauralee was pleased with the dignity of all her fellow campaigners.

She was pleased, too, that Jim walked home with them, planning their route so that her home was the last stop. They stood out front exchanging pleasantries until the front door opened and Binky put his head out and yelled, "Why don't ya come in? You'll freeze to death out there."

Lauralee turned and said in honeyed tones, "Why, Binky, I didn't realize you were so concerned about me."

"I'm not," he yelled back. "I just don't want your frozen

bodies blocking the sidewalk in the morning." And with a raucous snort he shut the door again.

Lauralee shrugged at Jim. "He's a trial," she said resignedly.

"Yeah, I know," Jim grinned. "I've got one just as bad only it's a sister. I guess I better be going. See you tomorrow."

He sounded as though he was really looking forward to it, and the thought made Lauralee glow as she entered the house. Inside, Binky's head appeared over the banister.

"Better not let Bud see ya with that guy," he warned.

Lauralee looked up. "And why not?" she asked archly.

"He kinda likes ya, too."

She could have kissed old Bink then, she felt so good. Imagine, two men fighting over her!

Jenny's letter was a bit more cheerful today, too. She had been invited to a party and was going with the boy next door.

"Not that I'm crazy to go with him," she wrote in the old independent-so-far-as-boys-are-concerned way. "But it's a date affair so I don't have much choice."

The next meeting of the candidates on the Popular Party ticket was at Annie David's house. Lauralee looked forward to that with pleasure, yet with some misgivings, too.

Many times she had passed the gloomy-looking Victorian mansion, set back in a grove of ancient trees, where Annie lived with her widowed mother and aunt in a state of virtual isolation. But she had never been inside it.

What would the house be like inside? She had always thought it must be something like the setting of a Boris

Karloff movie—dark, dim and mysterious. It took some fortitude on her part to walk up the stone steps onto the wide porch that swept around the front and one side of the many-gabled structure. The bell seemed to tinkle from inside a cavern as she and Elena waited.

Annie opened the door—and the hallway into which they stepped was anything but ghostly.

"This is my mother," Annie said shyly. Mrs. David was pale and frail but she was friendly enough. "My friends Lauralee Larkin and Elena Sloshek." Annie's voice seemed to linger on the word "friends."

"We are so glad to have you." Mrs. David smiled and she seemed genuinely pleased to see them. They all went into the living room and sat down on a sofa before a crackling fire in the marble-manteled fireplace. How cheerful it was, really, with a big bowl of golden mums on the low coffee table and the flickering light of the fire enhancing the sheen of satin-covered chairs!

They waited there until Jim arrived and then together they walked up a wide curving stairway to the third floor.

"This is my studio." Annie smiled as she led them into a small round room with windows all around. Lauralee knew it to be the top room of the turret that rose up from one side of the house.

"How perfect!" she cried as they walked in and saw a drawing table before a window, with shelves beneath, and a curved, velvet-cushioned seat. On a small table were colorful vases full of pens and pencils and brushes, and the dark canvas-covered wall was hung with Picasso and Renoir and brilliant Van Gogh prints.

"Boy, I could get inspired to draw and paint in here," Jim said admiringly.

"I like it," said Annie and motioned them to the window seat.

Posters and campaign buttons were the day's project, and Annie lost no time in showing them the designs she had made. Several were clever, but the one they selected featured a silhouette of Lauralee's head, with smaller likenesses of her running mates grouped around it. Their slogan, "Hop to the Top With the Popular Party," was lettered in red at the top and "Vote the Popular Ticket" in blue at the bottom. It was simple, dignified, and effective.

They began working on the posters right away. Annie sketched in the silhouettes, and Elena filled them in with black ink. Jim, who had a flair for lettering, sketched in and outlined the printed matter, and Lauralee filled those in with paint.

While working, Lauralee took in every detail of Annie's cozy nook. Was this one reason Annie seemed so serene and content with her lot, doing the work she liked to do in such pleasant surroundings? The idea seemed logical. Still, Annie was no social recluse either, not by choice anyway. She liked friends around, seeming right now to be very glad they had come.

Did all charming people move in the so-called charmed circle? Lauralee was beginning to doubt it.

Mrs. David was sweet, too, bringing up a pot of hot chocolate, a plate of cookies, and mugs and trays, and then leaving them to their business.

Sipping the chocolate and watching shadowy leaves go

swirling down in the fast approaching dusk, Lauralee felt an exquisite sense of contentment. Eloise and Eileen and Marion were bright and gay and their company desirable, but Elena and Annie were good companions, too.

Elena, it seemed, was also enjoying the comradeship she had found among these classmates. Her dark eyes fairly glowed. She, too, was artistic and creative and in this group had found a delightful niche.

Lauralee remembered the beautifully painted furniture in the Sloshek home, and the embroidery, and decided to ask Elena to help her decorate an unpainted dressing table that Dad had just bought for her room. Perhaps Maxine was content to enamel hers pink and put a ruffly organdy skirt around the bottom but Lauralee wasn't—not after seeing the decorative effect of the painted pieces at the Slosheks'.

Tiny pink flowers with blue birds and green-leafed vines intertwined would make a pretty design, she thought now. Why, she thought, I'm getting a little artistic myself. Perhaps some of Annie's and Elena's talents will rub off on me! And that would be all to the good.

Again Jim walked home with her. Pure joy welled up inside her. Here she was soon to become president of her freshman class and walking beside a nice, attractive boy who had deliberately planned to see her home. Things were certainly going her way!

11

Landslide!

"Oooooh!" Lauralee awakened, panic-stricken. "I have a fever! My face is burning up."

She sat bolt upright in bed, staring wildly at Maxine. Her sister was already up and patting her pert nose with a powder puff.

"I can't go to school today, Max! I simply can't," Lauralee continued to moan. She added tragically, "Of all days to be sick!"

The puff stopped moving. Maxine glanced at her in the mirror. "Yes, isn't it?" she murmured.

Lauralee stared at her sister's back. "You don't believe me!" she cried, aghast. "You don't think I'm sick?"

Maxine turned slowly and gave her a long, searching look. "All that's the matter with you," she said with only a trace of sympathy in her voice, "is that you have a bad case of election day jitters." She turned back to the mirror and lightly touched her lips with a pale lipstick.

Lauralee shut her eyes tight, then popped them open. Her own sister! So lacking in feeling. Then cold reason took over. Maxine *was* right after all, she wasn't really sick. She was simply fighting a wild, mad impulse to chuck the whole thing, simply not show up.

"Why did I ever let myself in for it?" she moaned silently to herself. "How could anyone in her right mind do such a thing?"

She squeezed her eyes shut again and before her swam a sea of faces—familiar faces every one, and they were all laughing at her as she stood on the stage of the school auditorium trying to make her speech. Instead, her tongue was stuck to the roof of her dry mouth and she could not utter a sound!

"Ohhhh!"

She slid down beneath the covers. How warm and cozy it was there! Could she make her mother believe she was sick? If so she could stay home, in bed all day, reading and listening to the radio while Mother brought up her meals on a tray! The prospect sent her into raptures of joyful relief.

She didn't want to be president of anything, ever.

"Oh, come on now, Lee." Maxine gently pulled down the covers. "It isn't as bad as all that. Why, once you're up there on the stage and have said a few words you will find yourself as cool and calm as a cucumber. Remember, I went through it in my sophomore year."

Lauralee eyed her blankly. "But you *were* as calm as a cucumber," she said accusingly.

Maxine shook her head and laughed. "I might have looked that way, on the outside," she said. "But underneath I was shaking like a leaf."

Lauralee sat up, her mouth a round O. "*You* were shaking

like a leaf?" she demanded. "Like I am now?"

"I certainly was," and Maxine pulled the covers clear off the bed.

For a second Lauralee sat there and shivered, though at the same time she felt strangely better. If Maxine could live through it, so could she.

"But I'll never run for another office," she vowed grimly as she slid out of bed. "Never so long as I live."

Maxine laughed at that, too, but she did help Lauralee get herself together and straighten up her side of the room. She also helped her remember the books and notebooks she would need that day. In spite of her sister's reassurance, Lauralee's mind was far from such mundane matters.

On the stairs she felt giddy and weak. She was glad that Dad's face was hidden behind his newspaper, Mother was in the kitchen, and Binky hadn't come down yet! If anybody should mention what day it was, she'd fly apart.

Mother came in then with a platter of bacon and eggs in one hand and a plate of warm, buttered toast in the other.

"Good morning, girls," she said as usual.

"Hi, Mom," Lauralee managed to greet her weakly.

Dad came from behind the paper and began to serve the bacon and eggs. He put a small portion on Lauralee's plate, apparently knowing she wouldn't eat much this morning. It was a good thing nobody insisted that she eat. She couldn't have forced a bite of food down if she had tried ever so hard. She did manage a sip of milk though.

Later when Dad rose to leave he did say, "Well, good luck, campaigner," and tried to be jovial about it, ignoring the stricken look on Lauralee's face when she turned toward him.

But Binky, grinning fiendishly, blurted out, "Boy, with her speech she'll need it!"

Mom's "Binky!" quieted him.

Lauralee looked at her brother reproachfully. She didn't wish him any bad luck but she just hoped that someday he found himself in her predicament.

Her steps to the corner bus stop were slow and reluctant. On the way she tried mentally to run through her speech. Horror swept over her. She couldn't even remember the opening line! Again she fought the impulse to turn around, go back home, and forget the whole thing.

Tammy Taylor came up and greeted her. Lauralee noticed that Tammy wasn't wearing the campaign button she had given her two days ago, the one with "Vote the Popular Ticket" on it. She and Binky had cut a million of those out of cardboard, it had seemed, and put the letters on them, and a safety pin on the back with cellophane tape. Tammy had worn it yesterday on the lapel of her coat. Had she forgotten it this morning? Or had she decided to vote for somebody else?

"Hi, Tammy," she greeted her now, hoping Tammy hadn't noticed her eying the spot where the button should be. It wouldn't do to antagonize a prospective supporter.

Wearing the buttons probably wasn't important this morning anyway. The buttons and posters, displayed in the cafeteria and everywhere else throughout the school where they were allowed, had already done their duty, whipping up interest in the Popular Party. It would be the speeches this morning that would bring in the winning votes. Speech! She felt dizzy again.

Two other girls came up, chatting and laughing. They greeted her just as though it was a day like other days. How could they be so cheerful this morning? But then, they hadn't been foolish enough to run for class offices; and they didn't have to get up on a stage and make speeches.

Bud appeared, a big ear-to-ear, high-humored grin on his face. If he had a care in the world it didn't show. Approaching Lauralee he struck up a fighter pose.

"Put up your dukes," he bantered laughingly. Then, just as quickly, he pulled a long, solemn face. "It was a good fight, Ma, but I lost."

A shriek of laughter from the others followed. But Lauralee didn't think it was funny. "Ha, ha," she muttered and turned away.

"I was just joking." Bud was contrite.

"Some joke." She refused to be placated.

Still, if his speech and those of his running mates were as silly as his attitude this morning, she thought, watching him tip his ridiculous red hat down almost onto his nose and then stagger around as though he couldn't see, the Mavericks didn't stand a chance of winning the election.

Feeling a little better, she got onto the bus. The others seemed to sense her desire to be alone and left her so—all except Bud! All the way to school perfectly inane remarks bounced to and from him and all around the bus. It was disgusting, Lauralee thought, as she silently went through her speech without a hitch.

Elena and Annie met her in front of the school. They

looked a little white around the mouth, too, and tense.

"I'll be so glad when it's all over with," Annie said, rolling her eyes skyward.

"And I, too," said Elena with feeling.

Lauralee was brisk now. "Oh, it won't be so bad. Why, after you've said a few words you will start feeling as calm and cool as a cucumber."

"I hope you're right," said Jim, as he came up behind them. A big campaign button was pinned to the front of his sweater, and then Lauralee noticed for the first time that Elena and Annie were wearing theirs.

"Where's yours?" Jim tapped his button and looked at her. Lauralee gasped. She had forgotten to wear hers!

"Oh, dear," she wiped a tear of laughter away, "what an absent-minded president I'll make."

That broke the tension within her—for a while.

"I'm taking this much too seriously," she thought.

But minutes before the third period, panic again took possession of her. For one brief moment she wished the school would collapse and bury her in the debris!

"It's like I'm walking in my sleep," she whispered to Elena as the freshman class filed into the auditorium, and the two girls took their seats together in the front row.

"Me, too," Elena smiled nervously.

Jim and Annie just looked at her mutely and accusingly, as though she alone had gotten them into this—which was true, she thought miserably.

She looked down the row where the candidates of the other three parties sat. With some satisfaction she noticed none of them looked perfectly at ease either; even Bud seemed almost grim, as though he were trying to remember just what he was going to do once he was up on that stage.

Harry Lawton, his sidekick and a clown if ever there was one, was making a big effort to appear nonchalant. What in the world did they have those gaudy handkerchiefs tied around their necks for? Oh, yes, their party was called the Mavericks and it was supposed to have a sort of Western touch, she supposed.

There was Robert Lee, and he was the only one who looked anywhere near normal. Their eyes met and he winked at her. It didn't make her feel all fluttery this morning but it did lift her spirits a bit, temporarily. She even managed to wink back, knowing that this mannerism of his meant absolutely nothing. He winked at everybody!

But that drawl was going to be stiff competition, especially among the girls. It was a mean advantage he had but there was nothing anybody could do about it.

Her gaze rested on Susan Harris. "She's as scared as I am," she thought jubilantly. "And she's a cheerleader, and used to being before crowds."

But leading a cheer and making a speech were two different things; she knew that, too.

At the same time her hopes of winning the election took a nose dive. For the first time she saw all her opponents together, and the sight was overwhelming—especially Sam Tabor, sitting with arms folded and steel-gray eyes unwavering on one of the chairs that were placed on the stage. He looked so dignified and sure of himself. What a president he would make! She could see his picture in the yearbook now on the page reserved for freshmen class officers!

All four of the Astronaut candidates sat with homemade space helmets resting on their laps.

"Wonder what kind of a skit they will put on," she whispered to Elena.

Elena shrugged, then put one finger on her lips. The principal, Mr. Callison, strode onto the stage. As if by magic the chattering and giggling and movement in the hall quieted until one could have heard a feather drop.

"As all of you know," he said smilingly, "we have come here to attend to some important business—election of class officers." He went on to tell about fair play and how the desires of the majority should prevail in this example of democratic election.

Then, with just the right blend of solemnity and good humor—a trait that made him extremely popular with the entire student body—the tall, graying man introduced the president of the Student Council, Raymond Haskill. Raymond was a poised and polished senior.

"Each of you," Raymond began smoothly, "received a slip of paper when you came in. After the campaigning is over, write your choice for each of the four offices on it, fold it, and hand it to the monitors on your way out."

He paused and then continued, "Thirty minutes is all the time allowed for speeches, skits, and voting. Each of our four parties is allowed equal time, to be used as its candidates see fit." He consulted a piece of paper in his hand. "Will the candidates of the party called the Experts come forward?"

Sam Tabor arose, tall, dignified, and determined. He went up onto the stage, followed by Robert Lee Morton, walking with easy grace. Then came Sally Buskirk, who was running for treasurer.

That was their mistake, Lauralee thought, putting Sally on their ticket, for she was a conceited little show-off. However Tina Terrill, in their secretary slot, wasn't so bad.

Sam's speech was a nice blend of dignity and humor and sincerity. Robert Lee's was short and to the point. Sally giggled all through hers and completely destroyed the effectiveness of their efforts. Tina's was a lame effort to cover up for Sally.

"Unless the Astronauts come up with something pretty tremendous," Lauralee thought smugly, "we're in." She had no Sally Buskirk on her team, thank goodness.

The members of the Astronaut party went up onto the stage next. Susan was a little nervous at first but after they had put on their helmets and started to sing the little song that started their skit, her cheer-leading ability came to her aid and she did better.

The realization that the Popular Party had to go up there next jolted Lauralee. She became so jittery that everything happening on the stage became blurred. She knew only that, instead of speeches, each Astronaut recited a funny little rhyme telling what he or she would do if put into orbit as a class officer.

Head down, breathing deeply, clasping and unclasping her hands, Lauralee waited tensely. A roar of laughter suddenly poured out over the auditorium and jerked her to attention. One of the Astronauts, while gesturing, had lost his helmet. Mr. Callison, grinning, was handing it back to him. She saw it was Dave Foxe, and he was laughing so hard he forgot to look to see which was the front of the helmet and put it on backward. This caused more laughter.

As the Astronauts came off the stage, still giggling, the thought ran through Lauralee's mind, "They will never win. Their skit didn't live up to the name of their party."

Then, before she knew it, she and Elena and Annie and Jim, in that order, were on their way upstage. Her legs felt like matchsticks. Somehow she managed to reach one of the chairs and sit down on it.

The sight of all those faces out there made her feel as if she had seen a ghost. Moistening her lips, she stared down at the row of unlit footlights and sat rigidly erect.

One by one Raymond announced them, and each stood up. Lauralee was last.

She walked stiffly to the lectern and laid her handwritten speech on it. She had no intention of looking at the speech, having carefully learned it by heart, but putting it there gave her something to do while she gathered her courage.

She opened her mouth. From out of somewhere came a voice that startled her.

"Fellow classmates," came the strange voice, "I stand before you today—" It was *her* voice! Heaven forbid! She gulped and went doggedly on, "—asking you to elect me president of our class for this coming year—" she paused for dramatic effect, "our freshman year."

There the first few words were out. She should be in complete control, but she wasn't. Her knees shook horribly and, while speaking one line, she groped ahead for the next. Suppose she got them mixed? The thought put a decided tremor in her voice. Then she looked down at her audience. There seemed to be thousands and thousands listening to her. She felt hot and cold as she shrilled out her past accomplishments.

Now, in the telling, they seemed so silly.

She gulped. "If elected I promise to work hard"—in her effort to emphasize the last word she squeaked—"for better relations between students and parents and teachers"—she hurried now—"to further the work of the Student Council and. . . ." When the last word was out it seemed to her as if she had been speaking for at least an hour. Limp as a rubber band she went back to her seat beside the others. They all went off the stage.

The stage was all set for the Mavericks. No longer tense, Lauralee sat back to enjoy watching Bud suffer.

Bud and his three running mates rose. With a rebel yell mingled with an Indian war cry that shattered the acoustics of the auditorium they bounded up the steps to the stage.

An electric sense of expectation ran through the audience. What do we have here? it seemed to say. Everybody sat back, pleasurably awakened.

They weren't disappointed. Wearing ten-gallon hats, whipped from nowhere, the Mavericks walked onto the stage with the exaggerated rolling gait of cowboys long in the saddle. Their bright shirts, blue Levis, and toy holsters holding pop-pistols heightened the comic effect. Each picked up one of the chairs, turned it around and sat down backward with arms folded over the back.

"How absolutely corny!" Lauralee sniffed. But this could be expected from Bud and those three clowns he had put on his ticket.

Jack Meyers, a tall, gangling fellow running for secretary, was introduced first. With thumbs hooked into the belt of his holster, he swaggered to the front of the stage. Giving a bashful, Will Rogers-type grin, he said, " 'Lo."

This brought down the house. Jack just stood there grinning until the howl quieted down. Then he opened his mouth. But before a word came out the howl started again, for from out of the wings had come a prancing calf. The front half of the cloth and papier mâché costume was filled by one boy and the other half by another and it was hard to tell which half was enjoying it the most.

The front half opened its large mouth, rolled its huge round eyes, and bellowed, "Mooooo!" The back half, at the same time, swung the rope tail in a complete circle! Bud, properly horrified, lassoed the critter and dragged it off stage.

It came right back on again, followed by three masked bandits. This kept up while all the candidates were speaking. No one heard a word of what they said, but it didn't seem to matter because everyone was laughing so hard.

Of all the campaigns! Lauralee laughed right along with the others. Now she was certain the Mavericks wouldn't win a single office.

An hour later the results were heard over the inter-com system. The Mavericks had won by a landslide!

12

Good Loser

Frowning, Lauralee went down the long first-floor corridor and out of the school. She looked neither to the right nor the left. "I don't want to talk to *anybody!*" she thought fiercely.

Never in her whole life had she felt so humiliated. Every vote cast for the Mavericks had been a vote *against* her.

Friends! Ha! That was a laugh. The only true friend she had ever had was Jenny. From now on she would remember that and act accordingly. No more of this outgoing, gregarious stuff for her.

"If anybody speaks to me, I'll scream!" she vowed as, with head down, she stalked down the long flight of cement steps.

Elena was waiting at the bottom, a cheery smile on her rather broad, flat face. She touched Lauralee's sleeve.

"Let us walk home together, no?" she asked, as pleasantly as though nothing out of the ordinary had happened that day.

"No! No!" Lauralee wanted to shriek. But she took a firmer grip on her emotions and shrugged indifferently.

"If you want to."

Elena fell into step beside her and they walked a short way in complete silence.

Then Elena tried again. "It is a nice day, is it not?" she asked, lifting her own rosy face to the slight breeze and breathing deeply.

Lauralee bit back a sharp reply. What a brilliant observation! *Anyone* could see the weather was nice, bright and sunny and crisp. But the *day!* It had been anything but nice and Elena should know that as well as anybody.

"Ummmm," she muttered, hoping to shut off the girl's silly chatter.

"You feel badly about the election, no?" she asked, as they went toward Willow Avenue, their feet making crispy, crackly sounds on the fallen leaves.

Lauralee sniffed. Another brilliant observation. "Well," she said more sharply than she had intended, "I don't feel exactly *good* about it."

Elena bit her lip. "It was I," she said softly, a catch in her voice, "who lost the election for the Popular Party."

Lauralee jerked her attention up and away from the toes of her flats. Her eyes were wide with surprise. Elena realized that, too? Right after the results of the voting had been announced, Lauralee had come to the conclusion that she hadn't been very bright in choosing her running mates.

Elena *had* looked queer up there on the stage, with her too-big, ill-fitting clothes and heavy shoes, and the braid of hair wrapped around her head like a rope. To boys and girls who put such a high value on sharpness, she must have seemed pretty poor material for a class officer.

"Oh, I wouldn't say that," she replied, "exactly."

Annie hadn't helped any either. She had been awkward and painfully shy while making her speech. Jim had been disappointing, too, now that she looked back at it. Why, of all days, had he chosen this one to wear that tacky old gray sweater, when she knew he had a half dozen really sharp ones?

She had done pretty well herself, she had decided—a bit nervous at first but poised and polished after the first few lines of her speech. And dignified, she had been that, too, and well dressed.

Elena seemed to have tuned in to her wave length.

"I should never have run on any ticket," she said, "a queer-looking foreigner like me!" She could have added, "But you talked me into it," but she didn't.

Lauralee was fully aware of that. "And if I had it to do over again, I wouldn't!" she thought even more fiercely.

She only said, "Well, there's not much sense in crying over it now." And to show an indifference she did not feel she laughed hollowly.

And she wasn't going to cry over it either. She was going to forget the whole thing. There was just one thing for certain and that was she would never put herself into such an embarrassing position again!

Outgoing and friendly—phooey! All a person needed was one friend and she had that. Tonight she would go home and write a long letter to Jenny.

She and Elena parted later in gloomy silence.

Now the only thing she had to dread was what her parents would say about her defeat. Would they drown her with sympathy? She hoped not. Would they treat the whole thing as a big joke? It hadn't been. Would they be disappointed in her?

Bud and three boys went by in an old car driven by Ted Harris, a junior. They yelled at her good-naturedly and she waved back, determined not to let *them* even guess how she felt.

"How silly Bud and the rest of his party looked and acted," she thought bitterly. "But then they could get away with it. Everybody knows they can act and look as sharp as sharp when they want to." She kicked a pile of whirled-up leaves and added to herself, "They knew, too, that Elena and Annie never look any different than they did up there on stage."

Of course, the class wouldn't want officers like them. How could she have been so stupid as to think so? Quietly she slipped through the front door of her home.

" 'Lo," Binky said, not even looking up from his prone position on the living-room floor. He was busily putting together the pieces of one of his numerous do-it-yourself kits. The results ranged from models of battleships to those of ancient cars, and Mother often wondered why it seemed the only place he could work was on her new carpeting. But today, Lauralee noted, he had placed a layer of newspapers under his work.

"Letter from Jenny!" He waved toward the hall table with a brush full of the glue he had been smearing on one tiny piece of wood.

"Oh, fine!" Lauralee replied, thankful that he hadn't said a word about the election. And, judging from the absorbed way he held his lower lip beneath his two large front teeth, one would think he hadn't known a thing about it. And after all the campaign buttons he had cut out of cardboard for her!

Lauralee picked up the letter. Through the doorway she saw Mother, busy in the kitchen, and held her breath.

Mother looked up from the crust she was deftly rolling for the individual casseroles of chicken pies lined up before her. She smiled and said, "Hello, dear. My, that looks like a nice fat letter from Jenny. Go on upstairs and read it. I have dinner ready to pop into the oven."

"Thanks, Mom," Lauralee replied gratefully. She fled up the stairs and into the room she shared with Max. Thank goodness, Max wasn't home yet. She could catch her breath before she had to face her sister.

Sitting on the edge of her bed she stared down at Jenny's letter. How was she ever going to answer it? Could she bring herself to tell Jenny of her stinging defeat, especially after her glowing letters telling about the campaign, so full of her confidence in victory?

What an ecstatic letter she had planned to write this very afternoon! She shuddered at the thought.

Slowly she tore open the letter from California. With a sinking heart she read it through. More and more, she realized sadly, she and Jenny were drifting apart, becoming strangers to each other.

Jenny's letter was so short! The fatness had come from a couple of newspaper clippings telling of things that were happening in her school there. Jenny Moore's name, mentioned twice, was heavily underscored with red crayon and the other names were those of boys and girls Lauralee didn't know and cared nothing about.

A wave of longing for Jenny swept over Lauralee, threatening to engulf her. But it was for the Jenny who had lived in Elm Park, not the one who had sent this letter.

Maxine burst in then, her face a rosy glow both from the cold outside and the fact that Wayne had driven her home in his dad's car.

"And we have a movie date Saturday night," she said dreamily.

Lauralee looked at her sister in downright reproach. How could anyone be so happy? But then everything always worked out right for Maxine.

"Oh, dear, where's my old gray skirt?" Maxine's head was in the closet and she was rummaging through the long line of skirts and dresses hanging there.

"It's right in front of you!" Lauralee said, coming up behind her sister and taking the skirt off its hanger. "No wonder you can't see anything with all those stars in your eyes."

She wasn't going to let Max think she was downhearted.

"Oh, how you talk, Lee!" Max laughed, pleased. A few minutes later she was off downstairs, after telling her sister that even though it was Lauralee's night to set the table she would do it. Not one word did she say about the election either, and Lauralee knew that she knew the results.

But of course! Mother and Binky and Max were purposely ignoring the subject to spare her feelings!

"Mighty decent of them," Lauralee told herself dejectedly. Then she spied a rough draft of her campaign speech lying in a drawer of her desk. Taking it out she tore it to shreds and threw it into the wastebasket. Well, she wouldn't mention the sorry thing either.

But Dad brought it up later, just as they were finishing dessert. Looking straight at her he said solemnly, "We're proud of you, kitten."

Lauralee's chin almost dropped into her baked apple. Dad had called *her* kitten! Then she looked up. What kind of a joke was this anyway? Then she noticed the pleased-with-themselves expressions on the faces of Mother and Max and Binky.

"Proud? Of me? What on earth for?"

"For being such a good loser."

While the others beamed at her, she gulped. Good loser! Why, she was anything but that! She had blamed everything and everybody for losing the election, except herself. A sense of shame engulfed her. But her family didn't know that and somehow she was glad she hadn't spouted off her thoughts, really, to anybody.

If they thought she was a good loser, well, then, she'd try to be one. "Oh, that," she shrugged. She forced a bright laugh that she knew sounded rather tinny. "Can't win 'em all, as Binky says."

Binky beamed at being quoted.

"That's the spirit," Dad said warmly. "And just to celebrate the event and all you've learned from it, your mother and I and Max and Binky have decided to give you a sort of—well, very impromptu affair that we are calling a Good Loser party. How do you like that?"

"When?" she asked weakly.

"Tonight!" Binky grinned, adding, "While you were

upstairs Dad and Max took turns calling up all the freshmen who ran for office today."

Dad nodded. "Winners and losers."

Binky went on. "And they're all coming!"

He puckered his impish face into one of those comical expressions that usually made her laugh. But not tonight.

However, she would not let any of them know how she really felt.

Dad rose then. "Come on, Bink," he said. "Let's get to work on the recreation room."

They clattered down the stairs and Lauralee knew it was to remove the leftover paper and paints and such from all the campaign posters and buttons that had been made there.

"Max and I will take care of the dishes, dear, and clear up the kitchen," Mother said. "You go upstairs and get ready to greet your guests. They'll begin arriving in an hour or so."

Lauralee rose reluctantly. Dad and Mom never let an excuse for a party go by without having one, but this was ridiculous. Still she smiled, though it made her cheeks ache to do so, and did as she was told. She put on her best red wool skirt and sweater to match. She brushed her hair until it gleamed and powdered her nose and put on a touch of lipstick. Then she made a face at her reflection in the mirror and went down to the living room.

Sam Tabor arrived first.

"Wanta weep on my shoulder?" he demanded with a big grin as he came into the hallway. In spite of herself Lauralee had to squeal at sight of the big, bulging pad he wore on his shoulder underneath his sweater, giving him a strange, lopsided look. "I came prepared for a lot of it," he added, patting the lump.

"What a wonderful idea!" Lauralee cried and leaned over until her face was buried in what seemed to be a small pillow—and was.

"Boo, hoo!" She gave a synthetic sob.

Sam laughed. "Now I'll weep on your shoulder!" and he leaned over and boo-hooed. If Sam was bothered by defeat one would never guess it. Nor did he look hang-dog or humiliated.

Had she, perhaps, taken the whole thing too seriously?

The bell rang again and she opened the door and Bud Newton came in. Sam raised a hand and shouted, "Hail the conquering hero!"

"This is a real mixer," Dave Foxe said later, admiringly.

"It shuah is," agreed Robert Lee. "Ah've met moah people tonight than Ah have in all the time since school stahted."

Pleasure welled up in Lauralee. Dad and Mom had known what they were doing all along. But didn't they always?

Elena and Annie came together and were shy at first— but not after Lauralee made a determined effort to see that they joined in the festivities. Even so, Elena again spoke of what she thought was the major part she had played in the failure of the Popular Party.

"Oh, come on now, Elena." Lauralee put an affectionate arm about Elena's shoulders. "If anyone is to blame, I guess I am that person. I insisted that everything be so stiff and what I thought was dignified." Her eyes followed Bud now dancing around the floor with Annie. "I know now that one can be—well, light-hearted and still be sincere."

Elena smiled happily as though a big load had been lifted from her shoulders. She went back to a group in one corner and told a funny Moravian folk tale that sent them all into gales of laughter.

For the next few hours the recreation room rang with the sounds of gay talk and laughter, games being played, and dancing. While refreshments were being served the conversation swerved to coming events at school—such as Stunt Night and Homecoming.

"Ah'm going to play mah git-tahr," Robert Lee drawled, "and sing, and that will be the stunt to end all Stunt Nights."

That brought laughter but not the razzing kind. Some had heard Robert Lee strum and sing his folk songs and they knew he was pretty good.

Lauralee stopped before him with a plate of Mom's brownies.

"I wish I could sing or something," she said lightly. "I'd like to audition for Stunt Night, too."

She wanted to get right back into the swim of things. Not having won the election, she wanted to find some other way to distinguish herself.

Stunt Night offered a fine opportunity to everyone with a talent for entertaining. It was an important event, the only money-making one of the year, and for a worthy cause. The proceeds from the sale of tickets went into the fund that financed the round-trip fares of the foreign exchange students invited each year to Willowlake.

Any student could audition for Stunt Night before the Student Council if he or she or a group could sing or dance, play instruments, put on a skit, or give impersonations.

This year it had been announced as a sort of talent hunt affair, each act to be sponsored. Prizes would be given for the best, the funniest, and the most original offering in several categories. The winners always had their pictures in the local paper.

"Y'all will think of something," Robert Lee encouraged her now.

Lauralee shook her head. "No, I won't," she replied moving on with the brownies. "I can't put on a stunt and I have no one else I can sponsor."

Then, before she knew it, the evening was over.

"Oh, I had a wonderful time!" She heard that over and over as her guests took their leave. Elena squeezed her hand tight and Annie's eyes glowed.

"Honestly," Lauralee said later, "you couldn't tell the winners from the losers."

"And that's the way it should be," said Dad. "Just remember that for every winner there is a loser. The only sure way to avoid losing is never to do anything, and who wants to live in a vacuum? Besides we learn more from our failures and mistakes than from our successes. So, as the old saying goes, there is no loss without some gain."

And he was absolutely right, Lauralee thought as she went happily to bed. She had worked hard and lost the election. But she had learned that she could get up before a crowd and make a speech, and that she could organize things and get them done. And she had made many friends.

"Best of all," she thought sleepily, "I think I learned how to be a good loser."

13

Reflected Glory

How nice to be hailed in the halls and stopped for chats by her new friends, as well as by those she already had. Lauralee found it a heart-warming experience, adding much fun to her school days—especially now that plans for a gala Homecoming weekend began seething through the school, catching everyone up in a surge of excitement. The date was weeks away but there was much planning to be done and preparations to be made.

It would begin on Saturday morning with a big parade, to be followed in the afternoon by a football game between the Willowlake Demons and their traditional foes, the Addison Knights. The climax would be a dance in the school gymnasium, with a big name band supplying the music and the Homecoming kings and queens leading the grand march.

Most of the girls began at once to wonder about their dates for the dance, but not Lauralee. She wasn't interested in going to any dance with a boy, especially now that Jim Talbot was paying so much attention to Susan Harris. But, if there was some exciting part she could play in the festivities she would be happy to do that.

Of course, if Bud or Robert Lee or Jim or some nice boy begged her to go with him, she just might consider it.

She took ten Stunt Night tickets and sold them in no time; but so did lots of others so there was no particular luster added to her name or reputation by that.

"Of course," she pirouetted before her mirror while making a wry face at herself, "I could get elected freshman Homecoming queen!" She laughed aloud at such fantasy. "I'll be as old as Whistler's Mother before I'm *that* popular."

It was no secret that Eloise Fisher was pretty certain she would be elected queen and there were half a dozen boys popular enough to rate the votes for king.

One Friday morning, as she made her way toward homeroom, Annie stopped her in the hall.

"Do me a favor?" Annie asked.

"Any time," Lauralee replied cheerfully.

Annie smiled, pleased. She sounded proud, too, as she went on. "I have been made chairman of the committee to decorate the freshman float for the Homecoming parade." Lauralee nodded. Annie was a natural for that job with her talent for designing and all. But what did that have to do with a favor from her? She soon found out when Annie asked eagerly, "Will you serve on my committee?"

Lauralee was momentarily taken aback. She wanted to take an active part in Homecoming activities but this wasn't exactly what she had in mind. Who ever heard of, or gave credit to, the people decorating a float? The chairman of the committee might be recognized for her effort but not the ones doing the hard work of putting it together.

"I know it will mean putting in hours of hard work," Annie noted her hesitation and pleaded, "but—"

"I don't have any artistic talent," Lauralee protested feebly.

"But you can organize and get things done like—well, like you did when we were campaigning."

Lauralee could not ignore that gentle thrust. How she had used her powers of persuasion to get Annie on her ticket— so she could make use of her talent for designing posters and such! How Annie had worked!

"Well, okay, I'll do the best I can," she replied trying to muster some enthusiasm.

Annie beamed. "Good," she said. "We're meeting this afternoon after school at my house."

So the trap snapped shut with Lauralee in it. Then the reaction set in.

"What a sap I am," Lauralee thought disgustedly. She had accepted a job that smart kids ducked. The other members of the committee were Helen Farley and Leslie Hayden—friends of Annie and art students also—and Elena Sloshek, she learned when the class bulletin was read a few minutes later.

But she was stuck with her promise and she knew it. Her state of mind wasn't helped any either when she heard Eloise remark, "Some float we will have with *that* crew in charge!"

The barb stung, so much so that Lauralee's indignation did a fast climb. Of all the nerve, Eloise talking about her and her friends like that! Did she think she and *her* friends were the only ones capable of handling such an important part of the class participation in the homecoming festivities? Well, Lauralee Larkin would show her! She would personally see to it that the freshman float was the most gorgeous thing in the whole parade.

But no spectacular ideas came up during the meeting that afternoon.

"The Homecoming theme this year," Annie informed them, "will be 'Hands Across the Sea,' in honor of our foreign exchange students. Somehow we must work the theme into the design of the float."

Then the talk veered to the problem of obtaining a truck on which to build the float and a garage big enough to build it in.

"Our garage is much too small." Annie was apologetic. So were the family garages of all the other members except Elena—the Slosheks had no garage at all. The meeting ended in agreement to work on those two problems and to be thinking of ideas for decorating the float.

When they met again at Elena's house, not much progress had been made.

"We'll have to do better than this," Annie said, real concern in her voice.

"We sure will!" cried Leslie. "Time's a'wasting."

"Doesn't anyone have any ideas at all, about the truck or the garage *or* the float?"

Lauralee spoke up then, half jokingly.

"I don't have a truck to offer or a garage," she said, "but in designing our float why can't we use a motif honoring our own foreign-born classmate?" And she pointed at Elena.

Annie clapped her hands in delight. All her creative nature needed was a tiny urge and it was off and spinning.

"Moravia!" she cried. "What a wonderful idea! We're not limited, you know, to Japan or Ireland, though I'll bet all the others will use those two. And they're good for barrels of ideas but—Moravia!" Her eyes went dreamy. "Their wonderful folk dances and art customs! There is a treasure house of ideas!"

The look on Elena's face grew brighter and brighter. Her foreign birth was not being ridiculed for a change! Instead it was being held up as something to be proud of!

Mrs. Sloshek understood enough English to know what they were talking about and that it would be good for her Elena.

"Wait, I show you something," she said softly. She put down the pot of chocolate and plate of *kipferdln* she carried and bustled from the room. She returned with an armful of glistening white starched stuff, fluted and flounced, with solid colors of satinlike materials gleaming like jewels in its folds.

Amid ooh's and ahhh's of the onlookers she shook it out. There emerged a beautiful peasant festival dress with short, full skirt and huge puffed sleeves, its bright bodice and overskirt richly embroidered.

"This I wore on special days when I was a girl in Moravia," she said, her plump cheeks dimpling with pleasure at the girls' admiration. "Put it on, Elena."

Elena slipped it on over the clothes she wore and, while bulky, it transformed her into an almost-beautiful creature. She puffed up the huge sleeves.

"These should be stuffed with paper," she giggled. "Then they look almost like wings."

Annie's eyes shone. "Can't you see that on the float?" she breathed.

Elena's eyes twinkled. Out of sheer exuberance she clapped her hands smartly and moved out into the big room. There she went into a whirling, toe-tapping, heel-clipping dance that left them all quite breathless.

"A Moravian folk dance," she said when she stopped.

An idea flashed through Lauralee's mind but it had nothing to do with a float.

"Teach me that dance, Elena!" she begged. "And I'll have Mother make a dress like yours and we can do it together for Stunt Night!"

How did she come by such a dazzling idea? The brilliance of it left her gasping. But would Elena consent to her plan?

Elena sank down into a chair, the skirt of the dress spread out all around her. Her dark eyes twinkled, pleased.

"Glad I will be to teach you!" she cried. "And to do the dance with you on Stunt Night."

The talk went back to the float but Lauralee's mind did not. All she could think about was the picture of herself whirling and twirling gracefully on the stage in a lovely dress like Elena's!

Mrs. Sloshek let her take the dress home. Mother exclaimed over it, too, and wrinkling her nose said, "Well, I couldn't possibly make one exactly like it, not in a year's time. All that embroidery. But I believe I can turn out one that might be considered a reasonable facsimile."

Lauralee gave her a happy hug. "Thank goodness for a

mother who can sew!" she cried. And she told her mother why she wanted it.

Mrs. Larkin's brow shot up. "Do you think you could learn such a dance? Remember, it comes much more naturally to a girl of Elena's temperament."

Lauralee smiled smugly. "I think I can learn what might be considered a reasonable facsimile," she joked.

After all, the dance consisted only of a few intricate steps and turns and, it seemed to her, a way of holding the hands against the hips, palms out, and a certain way of tapping the heels and toes. She could learn it easily. Already she could see her picture in the paper as a Stunt Night winner!

All aglow she went to her room. Then the telephone rang and Mother answered it and called, "It's for you, Lee."

"Hi, chum!" To her surprise it was Bud. With a rush of words he asked, "How's about going with me to the Sock Hop on the evening of the twenty-eighth—this month—October, that is?"

You could have knocked Lauralee over with the proverbial feather. She had heard rumors of a Sock Hop but hadn't given it much thought, up to this very moment. Now she gave it plenty.

Play it cool, Maxine had told her. She must not let Bud think for one minute that she was as pleased as she felt.

"Wellll. . . ." Then she panicked for a second. Stunt Night! Her eye flicked to a calendar beside the telephone. No, Stunt Night was the twenty-sixth. Then right out of a perfectly blue sky came another one of her brilliant ideas. Elena was such a *good* friend. "If you will get a date for my friend, Elena," she added.

She could almost hear Bud's consternation crackling on the other end of the wire.

"Sloshek?" he asked slowly, as though unable to believe what he had heard.

"Elena Sloshek," Lauralee repeated just as slowly. After all, if Eloise could make boy friends find dates for her friends, why couldn't she?

Bud gave a low whistle. Then he said, "I know I'm good, but I'm no magician."

"Elena is fine company."

"I don't doubt that," he agreed. "But to get her a date! Well, since you're twisting my arm, I'll turn on the old charm and give it a try."

"That's sweet of you, Bud." She was charming, too.

"Aw, c'mon, now!" Bud exploded. "What's this making like a movie star bit?"

She giggled and they chatted on for a few more minutes. When she hung up Lauralee was amazed at her own audacity, and pleased, too, in more ways than one. Bud had *asked* her, of his own free will, to a dance and she had put a price on her acceptance. It gave her a feeling of real power.

A yell from downstairs interrupted this pleasant line of thought.

"Whassamatter, Lee," Binky cried, "can't you see?" Laughter followed. "Boy, I'm a poet and don't know it."

Lauralee winced and waited for the raucous cackle to subside. Then she asked with admirable restraint, "All right, Braino, what's the joke?"

"There's a letter from Jenny down here," Binky said in injured tones. "S'prised you missed it, that's the joke."

"Ohhh, I forgot all about looking for mail!" she cried and ran down the stairs. There on the table was a fat letter from her friend. Almost guiltily she snatched it up. She hadn't yet answered the one she had received two days ago.

What was happening to her anyway? It wasn't that she had forgotten Jenny, it was just that she had been so busy thinking about the float, and the Homecoming parade. And now with the Sock Hop and the dance to learn for Stunt Night— well, when would she answer this one?

"I'll do it this very night," she vowed, "come what may."

She slipped out the numerous pages and began to read Jenny's untidy scrawl.

"Oh, Lee," the very first line ran, heavily underscored, with a big blob of ink at the end. "I'm so glad you wrote about the Willowlake Homecoming! For you see that is the week our teachers are having a two-day meeting and school is out and it is also the week that Dad is making a business trip back for some kind of a convention or other. Hang on to your hat! As you know, Grandma has been out here for a visit so Dad and I and Grandma are flying back together! Just think, I'll be in Elm Park for Homecoming! Isn't that the most? I'm so excited I can hardly write!" Another blob.

The letter went on and on, but Lauralee just skipped over it. The news she read at first had left her almost numb with joy.

She dashed downstairs.

"Oh, Mother!" she cried. "Jenny is coming back! For Homecoming weekend!" She did a dance around the kitchen and whirled into the dining room where Max was setting the table. Then on into the living room where Binky heard the news. Then Dad came through the front door and she told him while he was putting his hat and topcoat into the hall closet.

Every one of them seemed as excited as she. Oh, this had been her day all right, one of those rare periods of twenty-four hours when everything had turned out *just right*.

But the next one wasn't, nor was the next—or the next.

Elena did her best to teach her the Moravian folk dance. But the steps were much more difficult to learn than they looked to be.

Several times, when whirling around in practice, she landed *kerwhop* on the recreation room floor—once when Binky was looking! She could hear him chortle for hours afterward.

"Well, *you* just try tapping the floor with one toe while you're clicking your heel with the other!" she had fumed.

"Think I'm crazy?" he had snorted and left her alone for a while.

To her chagrin she found that when she did do the footwork fairly well her hands weren't held just right, with palms out, or she wasn't tossing her head in abandon, like Elena did.

She tried and tried and tried.

Bud tried and tried, too, so he said, to get a date for Elena for the Sock Hop.

"The guys just hem and haw and say, well, they know she's a nice girl and all that but—" His voice would trail off apologetically.

"She's different," Lauralee finished for him.

"That is putting it nicely," he grinned.

Then, because Bud was an acquaintance of long standing and she could speak her mind to him without fear of making him angry, she launched into a discourse about conformity. "Does everybody have to be exactly like everybody else?" she demanded. "Suppose we were all blondes or all brunettes. . . ."

Bud waited until she had run down. Then he answered in an exasperatingly superior masculine way, "There's a lot in what you say, chum. But the guys won't buy it. They want to date a girl that's—well"—he threw Lauralee into a delightful tizzy—"sharp, like *you* are."

It was the first time anyone had ever called her sharp. She had always supposed that only girls like Maxine or Eloise were considered that. She knew that she was, different, too—which really proved her point that the jewel of attractiveness had many facets.

"Thank you," she said demurely. And then, not so demurely, she went on to say that he had just taken the words out of her mouth, that one could be different and still be—

"But not too different," he said with male logic.

She knew what he meant. Elena's hairdo, her over-long, too-full skirts, her heavy shoes. . . . She sighed. There must be something she could do.

Later she talked to her mother about it.

"Well, we will have to tread softly," Mrs. Larkin warned.

One afternoon, while Elena and Lauralee were practicing their dance downstairs, Mrs. Larkin saw her chance. The girls had decided on a dress rehearsal, Lauralee's dress having been finished a few minutes before.

As Elena slipped into her own peasant dress, Mrs. Larkin picked up the skirt she had just taken off. "I'll mend this little rip in the hem," she said.

"Oh, thank you, Mrs. Larkin," cried Elena, adding, "My mother does so little sewing."

Mrs. Larkin smiled and took the skirt to her sewing room upstairs. There she shortened it *and* trimmed down the sides.

"How different it looks," Elena said when she put it back on. And it did. It fitted!

She wore it next day and almost everybody noticed the difference. But Bud had no more luck in getting her a date.

"It takes time for such things to sink in," he said.

"I guess I'm not much of a matchmaker," Lauralee thought glumly.

She was beginning to think she was not much of a folk dancer either. But it took Binky to convince her of it.

She and Elena were practicing. Binky was watching, his little eagle-eyes missing nothing, and she knew it. She knew, however, that she had to become accustomed to an audience and Binky was probably no more critical than lots of those who would come to Stunt Night.

Around the room she and Elena whirled and whirled. When they stopped for breath Binky rose and said flatly, "A folk dancer you ain't, sis," and he stalked off upstairs.

Lauralee's first reaction was to throw something at her young brother. Then, suddenly seeing the whole thing in its proper perspective, she sank down into a chair and said, "He is so right." She sighed deeply.

"What do you mean?" Disappointment clouded Elena's

face. She had looked forward to taking part in Stunt Night.

"It means I'm going to bow out." Then she saw the stricken look on Elena's face and added hastily, "But only from the dance. I think it would be best for me to sponsor you and sort of pretend, like the others, that I discovered you." She smiled brightly. "That way I can still use the dress Mother made for me."

Elena's smile returned. "As you wish," she said.

Lauralee smiled wryly. In not objecting to her withdrawal from the dance Elena was agreeing to her own appraisal of her efforts—which was only being honest. She should have known better, anyway, than to try to steal somebody else's thunder.

They went upstairs then and Lauralee was really surprised at the relief she felt. They found Maxine before a mirror working on a new hairdo.

"Ooooh, I like that," Lauralee said as her sister swirled a fringe of bangs down across her forehead.

"It looks nice," Elena agreed wistfully. Then she looked into the mirror and shook her head, "I wish something could be done for mine. But my father does not want me to cut it."

Maxine shot a meaningful look at Lauralee. What a challenge!

"Let me try," she begged.

Elena did not have to be asked twice. She sat down eagerly and unwound the braids, which were not as long as Lauralee had supposed.

Maxine snipped a bit off the ends but not enough to say it had been cut. She then twisted it into a sort of put-up pony tail, with a wisp of bangs and two curls before the ears.

"Terrific!" cried Lauralee.

"Better it does look!" Elena's eyes hungrily drank in her reflection. With the heavy braids off the top of her well-shaped head, her oval face had taken on a beautifully exotic look.

The next day the boys did a double-take when they saw her in the halls.

"Can that be Sloshek?" their expressions asked. But Bud had no time, really, to get a date for her because everybody seemed to be rushing around getting ready for the evening, which was Stunt Night.

Later Lauralee and Elena waited nervously backstage for their cue to go on. Elena looked perfectly beautiful in her mother's dress, with the huge sleeves puffed out with crumpled tissue paper and her dark hair now flowing loosely about her shoulders. Lauralee guessed she herself looked pretty, too, judging from the low, admiring whistle Bud had given her when he had seen her in the dress Mother had made.

"Whither art thou going, pretty maid?" he had teased.

She had tossed her head and replied in kind, " 'Tis for thee to find out, my nosy lad."

Bud and Jim Talbot sat right in the front row out there in the auditorium, ready to snort and whistle and clap like crazy, and that was one reason for her nervousness. Another reason was that Mr. and Mrs. Sloshek were out there, too, sitting alongside Mr. and Mrs. Larkin and Binky.

"Oh, dear," Lauralee thought as she twisted her hands in her lap, "how do I get myself into things like this?"

She longed to be able to get up and flee the building.

But she had felt the same way on class election day. Remembrance stiffened her spine. The feeling was transitory and would soon be replaced with one of satisfaction in a job well done.

"And now our next sponsor"—the voice of the master of ceremonies, Jack Torrence, came to her and she blanched —"is Miss Lauralee Larkin. Will Miss Larkin come in, please?"

She walked on stage like one in a dream, though the murmurs of admiration for her costume did drift into her consciousness. She sat down at Jack's "desk."

Briefly she answered his questions and told how she had "discovered" her protégé. To her great relief the folk music record started on cue and out came Elena. And what a dramatic entrance *she* made! What an actress!

What a dancer, too! Elena became a fiery tornado of motion, clicking her heels and tapping her toes, the colors of her costume changing like the hues of a brightly-painted whirling top.

Then, with a spirited gesture of raised arms and snapping fingers she exited. The applause was deafening.

Proudly Lauralee rose and waited for Elena to return. They took a bow together. She had sponsored a winner and she knew it, and she was content to bask in her friend's reflected glory.

14

Foolish Goose?

After the program Elena and Lauralee started down the corridor toward the side entrance and the parking lot where Mr. Larkin had told them to meet him. The Slosheks had come with the Larkins and would go home the same way. The girls carried their costumes on hangers inside plastic bags which were slung over their shoulders.

"To market, to market!" Lauralee giggled happily. "Bud and Jim, I do declare! Want to help us carry our produce?" And jokingly she indicated the bag.

"That's what we came back here for," Bud said gallantly, "to help you ladies."

He took the bag from her and slung it over his own shoulder. Jim did the same for Elena who seemed surprised and pleased. She looked really sharp, Lauralee thought, in the gray wool dress Mrs. Larkin had fitted for her two days before, and in the coat she had shortened. Her hair looked lovely, swept back into the specially fashioned pony tail.

Jim seemed aware of it, too.

Bud's pace quickened and soon he and Lauralee were ahead of Jim and Elena.

"Jim wanted to ask Elena to go to the Sock Hop with him," he explained and Lauralee followed an impulse to squeeze his free hand affectionately. Bud looked surprised. "Why, I didn't know I meant so much to you, Lee." He grinned and squeezed back. "It was Jim's idea to ask Elena, too," he added, "not mine."

Elena's face was radiant with delight when she and Jim emerged from the school a couple of minutes later. When she introduced Jim to her parents it was plain to Lauralee that everything had been arranged.

The Slosheks liked Jim, too, and Lauralee was glad that she had played even a small part in bringing this happiness to her friends.

Elena had been declared a winner of the night and the photographer from the local paper had taken her picture with several other winners. Lauralee did not feel one twinge of jealousy.

Next day Elena was treated like Miss America. She was stopped in the halls and congratulated. Eloise Fisher and Eileen Thompson and Marion Avery expressed their admiration, much to Lauralee's surprise. And so did Robert Lee and several other boys.

Elena was shy in accepting their congratulations; but the new self-confidence that resulted was most attractive.

Jim Talbot told everyone he was taking her to the Sock Hop, the big topic of conversation for the next two days.

"Double dating with Bud and Lauralee," he casually let it be known.

The Youth Center, at which the Sock Hop was being

held, was a long, low brick building two blocks from the high school. It had been built by public-spirited citizens and thoughtful parents as a rendezvous for teen-agers, where they could go for evenings of wholesome fun. There were booths in which to sit and talk while sipping pop or hot chocolate, sold at cost from the fountain manned on a rotating basis by volunteer fathers. There were Ping-pong and pool and card tables, and games of checkers and dominoes and shuffleboard. There was also a floor for dancing and a jukebox in one corner, though sometimes, as on this evening, the music was supplied by small live groups.

Mr. Cummings, the paid director of the Youth Center, had arranged for a six-member jazz group called the Tune Twisters to play for the Hop.

"They were here last year," Lauralee had overheard a sophomore say, "and they were terrific."

Mr. Newton drove Bud and Lauralee and Jim and Elena to the Hop. It was plain there was going to be a record crowd tonight.

Jim was proud of his date, it was easy to see that.

"Clothes may not make a person," Lauralee thought as she had watched Jim and Elena come out of the Sloshek home, "but they certainly can make a difference."

Elena had worn just what Lauralee had suggested, and she looked as sharp as the next one. That afternoon Elena had asked her what to wear.

"I have a green silk party dress," she had said. "Would it be all right?"

"Oh, this isn't a dress-up party, Elena," Lauralee had replied. "Just wear the brown skirt Mom fixed for you and the pretty beige blouse you have. Blouse and skirt is what I'm going to wear. And flats."

As she and Elena entered the building now she was pleased to note they were dressed as most of the other girls were. And the boys wore bright shirts and corduroy trousers and white, thick socks that showed generously.

"I guess that's why it is called a Sock Hop," Lauralee said. "I can't think of any other reason."

She looked around for familiar faces and saw Eloise with Robert Lee. She felt no pang at all—but did Bud? If he did, he covered it well. Was the torch he had carried for the pretty redhead being dimmed a bit? Lauralee was enjoying herself so much she didn't worry about it one way or the other.

"You can't dance to *that*," said Bud. So he and Lauralee sat in chairs around the wall as did a number of other couples.

It was strictly a listening tune. Even Eloise and Robert Lee sat it out. Lauralee noticed that, even while talking to Robert Lee, the redhead sent arch glances Bud's way.

And once, just once, Robert Lee winked at her. But it did not make her feel all a'twitter as it once had, though it pleased her quite a bit. After all, she wasn't going steady and the more attention she got from different boys, the better.

"Look who's coming in!" Bud hissed in her ear.

She looked toward the door in time to see Annie David come in—with a boy! A Richard Rowe, whom they had seen in classes, but didn't know. Annie saw them and headed their way.

Bud and Richard soon were talking like old friends. Richard turned out to be a very witty young man who had just moved from Chicago out to the suburb. They lived on Crescent Hill, a wealthy section of Elm Park, but he seemed as common as an old shoe.

"Good pair," Bud remarked without malice after they had moved on. "Both eggheads."

"Nothing the matter with that," Jim grinned. "Though they will probably spend the evening discussing poetry and Picasso."

Jim was a sort of egghead himself.

The next tune was definitely for dancing though, as usual, most of the couples were reluctant to be first on the floor, except, of course, Eloise and Robert Lee—and, to everyone's surprise, Annie and Richard! Richard was a good dancer, too.

The Tune Twisters had to leave at ten-thirty, in time to catch a bus back to the small college fifty miles away where they were students. The party began to lag after that.

"Say," said Bud, "how's about a gang of us going to somebody's house and finishing up the evening? There's a howl of an old movie on TV tonight—Ramon Ramondo in 'Desert Sheik' or something like that."

"Ooooh, I love those funny old movies!" one of the girls squealed. "They're so funny!"

Bud turned to the girls. "Whose house?" he asked.

Eloise came up then and Lauralee's suspicions as to her intentions rose. But they subsided when Robert Lee said, "Lauralee's. She's got the best rec room."

And he winked at her in a way that made Bud do a mockingly jealous scene which seemed to send Eloise into hysterics.

"I'll call home and see if it's okay with my folks," Laura-lee said lightly. She certainly felt popular tonight.

She emerged from the booth with her parents' full consent to their plan. "Dad will come for us," she said. She asked Annie and Richard if they would come, and they said they would. The group that converged on the coat-check room included Eloise and Robert Lee and Eileen and Marion and their dates.

Quite a group waited for the Larkin car. When it arrived Mr. Larkin's brows rose at the number. They couldn't possibly all crowd in.

Out of nowhere Mrs. Newton appeared. "Just thought I might be helpful," she laughed and some of them got into her blue sedan.

It was surprising what Mrs. Larkin could do on such short notice. The rec room had been readied, lamps were lit, the record player set up and a tub of ice had been filled with bottles of pop. On the tables were bowls of pretzels and cheese-flavored popcorn.

"Underprivileged kids, that's us!" Bud laughed as they went in.

The TV set was switched on and everyone sat around watching for a few minutes. Howls of laughter greeted the old movie and the heavily made-up actors with their stylized emoting.

Mr. and Mrs. Larkin gave up after watching a few scenes. "To think we used to enjoy those things," they said and went upstairs shaking their heads.

The set was soon switched off and records put on the player. After a little dancing, conversation became the order of the evening.

Everybody agreed that, so far, it had been a great year. Most said that high school was definitely more exciting than junior high. Lauralee hesitated on that.

"I liked junior high," she said dreamily. "I remember Jenny and I—" Jenny! Why, Jenny was coming to Elm Park for Homecoming and she hadn't even told anyone except the family about it! Most of the boys and girls here remembered a tomboyish, carefree Jenny.

"You two were thicker'n molasses in January," Bud remarked. "I remember that."

Lauralee's eyes twinkled. "And she's coming back!" she cried.

"Coming back? Don't the Moores like California?"

"Oh, yes. She is just coming back with her grandmother and dad, who has some business to attend to here."

For a moment Lauralee thought uneasily of that last letter of Jenny's lying unanswered on her desk. She had been *so* busy these last few days. Jenny was probably almost in tears wondering how fickle a bosom pal could be.

But Lauralee's contrition was short-lived—soon forgotten in the lively discussion of Homecoming and all the activities that would take place then.

The boys' big interest was the game with Addison.

"We'll wipe up the field with 'em this year," said Bud confidently. Robert Lee agreed enthusiastically and so did Jim. All three had been going out for practice but so far had been used only in scrimmage. But they knew all the first-string players by their first names and spoke of them as though they were close friends.

The girls were interested in the game, too, because the boys were. But they looked forward mostly to the dance. Then the parade came up for discussion, and that led to talk of the float and who would ride in it as king and queen.

Eloise dropped her lashes decorously. None of the other girls thought much of their chances. The boys pointed to each other as possible kings and each suggestion was greeted with hoots of laughter.

Annie then mentioned that the decorating committee had agreed to use Elena's homeland as a sort of motif for the float.

"But so far we haven't come up with any concrete ideas," she said lamely.

"Why not a peasant cart drawn by a donkey?" Richard laughed. "The king and queen could ride in that."

Annie's eyes sparkled. "The very thing!" she cried. "And Elena in her lovely dress could be one of their subjects!"

"Driving some paper geese beside the cart! On a field of green paper grass."

"With lots of garlands and flowers and fairy tale stuff!"

"Oh, Lauralee!" cried Annie "Do you have a big piece of paper and a pencil?"

"Of course." And Lauralee produced a piece of wrapping paper from a roll that Dad kept in the basement, and a black crayon. In no time at all Annie had produced a sketch of a two-wheeled, flower-bedecked cart with a dear little, flop-eared donkey drawing it. In the cart sat the freshman king and queen, with features purposely left out. But Elena was there, in her native dress, driving three geese beside the cart.

"And that," said Eloise in a voice ringing with sincerity, "is just *darling!*"

Then everyone present was sworn to secrecy about the whole thing, so it would come as more of a surprise in the parade. None of the other classes were letting it be known just what kind of a float they were building.

Mr. Larkin came down then with some giant pizzas cut into generous pie-shaped wedges.

The hour was late when the party broke up but, by shading her small desk lamp from Maxine's side of the room, Lauralee managed to stay awake long enough to answer Jenny's letter.

How happy she would be to have Jenny back, even if for only a few days, she wrote. She spoke glowingly of all the fun they would have with her new friends.

"Will Jenny like *that?*" she wondered. Should she leave out Bud's name, and Annie's and Elena's? Let Jenny believe it would be just the two of them as it had been before? *Could* it be? She folded the letter, sealed the envelope, and addressed it.

The decorating committee held another meeting the next Tuesday afternoon. Annie showed them a beautiful, finished sketch of the float, done in water color. Each member of the committee was enthusiastic about it.

"Now, we must get to work constructing it," Annie smiled. "First we'll need a garage big enough to build it in. Then we will need a truck to build it on, and last, and probably hardest to find, will be a cart sturdy enough for the king and queen to sit in."

Helen Farley spoke up. "My uncle's a building contractor," she said. "He told me he has a couple of trucks that aren't busy right now and we could have one of them for a couple of weeks."

"That's wonderful."

"I think, maybe, I can arrange for the garage," Elena said hesitantly. The others looked at her in surprise. The Sloshek house had no garage. "And maybe—" Elena decided to say no more. "I will know tomorrow."

The next day she did.

"Mr. Cramer," she announced, "told my father we could use his garage for to build the float in, and"—she puffed like a pouter pigeon—"he has a little pony cart his daughter used many years ago. We may use that, too!"

Amazement murmured through the group. Such priceless luck! And coming from the Cramers, who were generally considered pretty stiff-necked and distant.

"Will wonders never cease?" said Lauralee. "Our problems are solved."

"I'll say they are," agreed Leslie. "We could build a half dozen floats in that old coach house garage of the Cramers. The pony cart doesn't surprise me either. I've heard their place is stuffed with antiques like that."

"Well, all we want is some space. And there we will have it, thanks to Elena and her dad."

Work was soon begun. Helen's uncle sent the truck to the coach house. Every afternoon after that the committee gathered at the estate on the hill. They were greeted each time by a smiling, ever-helpful Mr. Sloshek.

The sides were taken from the truck, leaving the flat-bed. Chicken wire was put over the cab and bed and sides, to all but cover the wheels. Countless paper tissues, of various colors, were thrust into the mesh of the wire until the whole thing emerged looking like something out of fairyland. The bottom of the bed was green and the driver's section was covered with flowers and garlands.

The wicker cart was adorned with flowers and leaves, too, and set in the center of the bed. Then Annie produced a papier-mâché donkey she and Richard had made, gray and so lifelike one could almost see it lift its head and bray. Silken streamers were the harness and reins.

"I'll make the geese," Lauralee had volunteered.

Binky, who was surprisingly good at such things, helped her. He made chicken-wire frames, and they spent a whole weekend thrusting white tissues into the wire to simulate feathers. They made heads and feet of papier-mâché and painted bills and feet yellow.

There were times when Lauralee wondered why she worked so hard on the float. Annie would get the credit for its beauty and Elena would get to ride on it.

"I guess I'm the silly goose," she said as she stuck in the last piece of tissue.

Then Mother and Dad and Maxine came down and admired their work.

"It has been a lot of fun making them," she said, and Binky nodded.

She realized then that it *had* been lots of fun. So who cared about the glory and the credit?

15

Just We Two!

Lauralee's mood, upon awakening one morning the following week, was as changeable as the weather outside her window, dark and gloomy one minute and bright and sunny the next.

What exciting days lay just ahead—Jenny's visit and Homecoming weekend, with the parade, game and dance! Each was enough to send a girl into a spin, but all of them together!

Thank goodness she didn't have to worry about the float any more. It was finished except for putting those paper-tufted geese on it; and that was a minor job that could be done any afternoon or evening. Thoughts of the float brought a sigh of bliss from her. It was so beautiful. Sitting up and hugging her knees gleefully she mentally watched it slowly making its way down Elm Park's busiest streets. Wouldn't eyes pop at sight of it!

But then Eloise's snide little remark came back to her. "Some float we'll have with that crew in charge!" she had said. Well, she would change her tune when she climbed up into that lovely flower-decked cart to ride in state as freshman queen! For Lauralee was sure it would be Eloise who had that honor, with probably Bud as king. Those two seemed to pluck off all such plums.

"Though I'm not bitter about it any more," Lauralee thought now, resting her chin on her knees.

The vote for the Homecoming king and queen of each class would be taken next Thursday afternoon, last thing, and the results announced soon after.

"Well, I know one vote Eloise won't get," Lauralee remarked to no one in particular as she rolled over and gave her pillow a sharp slap of satisfaction. "Mine!" She winked at Goop, now sitting and glaring glassily at her from his vantage point atop her bedside table. "I'm going to vote for Elena."

There would be no candidates or campaigning or such in this election. Everyone would simply write down the name of the boy and girl of his or her choice, and the ones with the most votes would become the reigning monarchs for the festivities.

Lots of the boys and girls would vote for their best friends. It was strictly a popularity contest, with neither beauty nor brains a factor, though they certainly wouldn't be a drawback either. And Eloise would probably win.

"A lot I care about the queen bit." Lauralee rolled over the side of the bed then and tucked her feet into a pair of exaggeratedly fluffy mules. Looking down, she giggled at their size. Then, out of sheer exuberance she cried aloud, "And in a few days Jenny arrives!"

Maxine came into the room then, rubbing her already glowing face with a rough towel. "And aren't you the happy one!" she grinned at her sister fondly.

"You can say that again!" And Lauralee did a floppy-footed dance around the room holding Goop up high for a partner.

Deep down inside, though, she had her misgivings. The guilt she felt was a big, dark, fearsome cloud that occasionally blotted out her sunny feelings. She *was* glad Jenny was coming; she certainly wanted to see her old friend again, even if for only a few days. But at times she was apprehensive about the visit, too. Take the way she had felt last night, for example, when Bud had called.

"Either yes or no," he had said firmly. She couldn't blame him a bit, for he had been patient in dealing with her vacillating acceptance of his invitation to go to the Homecoming dance with him.

She really wanted to go to that dance, and she wanted to go with Bud, if for no other reason than to show off her newly acquired poise around boys. But she hesitated because of Jenny.

What would her friend say when she discovered that Lauralee had planned an important evening of her visit without her? But, Lauralee was inclined to argue, it was the only evening of the weekend that she would plan without her.

She and Mother were going to meet Jenny and Grandma Moore and Jenny's father at O'Hare field a week from today, Wednesday. At six-thirty in the evening the big jet on which they would come would be landing there. The next day she planned to take Jenny to school for a while and Saturday they would watch the parade together and then see the football game. Sunday afternoon Jenny and Mr. Moore were jetting back to California.

"Yes," she had gulped finally, knowing that if she didn't, Bud would ask another girl, a cute little blonde he was becoming friendly with lately. Robert Lee had already asked Eloise, she was pretty sure of that, and Jim had asked Elena, and Richard was taking Annie.

"About time," Bud had replied, a little miffed at her now. So, for the first time, she told him the reason for her hesitancy.

"Well, wait until Jenny comes," he had replied then in an expansive mood, "and if she says she wants to go to the dance, I'll see what I can do about getting *her* a date."

He emphasized the word "her" and, though Lauralee winced at the unflattering allusion to her friend, she knew that Jenny hadn't been the kind of girl that boys are crazy about taking out. She had been a little too sloppy-casual in her appearance, and a little too opinionated, and—well, a little too much of several things.

Still, the thought of hurting Jenny sent her into a slough of despair. Her very, very best friend—and, for a fleeting moment, she was certain it was Jenny and not Elena—would be hurt in not being included in each and every one of her plans, as of old.

She almost asked Bud to get a date for Jenny before Jenny came, saying that her friend would be glad to go. But would she? She was probably the same old Jenny, sneering at boys, dates, dancing, feminine clothes, and all the other things girls were interested in. A girl like that would make the boy she was out with pretty miserable, and Lauralee didn't want to do that to one of Bud's friends.

Of course, she admitted wryly, she had once felt the same way about boys that Jenny did, but that was a long time ago. She had changed, oh, so much. She sighed. She'd have a sweet time explaining *that* to Jenny.

Oh, well, she must get her mind back to things at hand. She began dressing for school. Dad had had to add his call to Mother's yesterday and it simply wasn't smart to let that happen two days in a row. She washed, brushed, and dressed briskly, and old Goop was resting comfortably in the center of a smooth bedspread when she closed the door and followed Maxine, by a surprisingly few minutes, downstairs.

The talk at the breakfast table centered on the coming week. One could almost believe that Mr. and Mrs. Larkin were students at Willowlake by listening to them talk about all its activities. Their interest was deep. Mr. Larkin took Binky to all the games in which Willowlake participated and was waiting for his son to go to the school and play on one of its teams.

And the float. . . . Both he and Mrs. Larkin had followed the building of it, almost tissue by tissue, and he said if it didn't take a prize he would personally take the matter up with the judges!

"Of course," he had chortled, "they might think I am prejudiced and throw me out."

Maxine was up to her ears in Homecoming plans, too. Wayne was taking her to the dance and she was part of a tableau on the senior float, though even Lauralee didn't know what. The seniors were keeping the theme of their float a secret, too. Her sister couldn't be queen this year, Lauralee knew that, for she had been queen in her sophomore year and it was an unwritten rule not to elect the same person to the same office twice during his or her high school career. It was a good rule, Lauralee thought; otherwise some girl like Eloise would take the same high honors year after year.

Lauralee looked at Max and a gasp almost escaped her when she saw the tiny gold football hanging on a chain around her sister's neck! Had Mother or Dad noticed it? If so, did they realize what it meant—that Wayne and Maxine were going steady? It had to be Wayne, for Tiny was strictly a basketball player.

If her parents had noticed it they kept it to themselves. But not Binky. "I see you're wearing old Wayne's football!" He grinned impishly at his oldest sister. "Mmmmm!" He puckered his lips and gave three loud, kissing smacks!

Maxine's eyes smoldered as she looked at him. Lauralee giggled in spite of her best intentions, and Dad's paper went up to hide a broad grin. Mother merely leaned over and said, "Binky!" in a reproving, though tolerant, voice.

But Binky had made his point and he was satisfied. He went back to his bowl of crispy, crackly cereal.

The incident had taken Lauralee's mind off Jenny for a moment and she was glad of that; but Mother brought it right back again.

"We must give a little party for Jenny while she is here," Mrs. Larkin said, pouring another cup of coffee for Dad, "and invite some of the boys and girls she and you used to know. Do you think that would be fun?"

Lauralee gave her mother a sudden look of sheer admiration and gratitude. This could be the solution to her problem.

"An open house!" she cried. "The very thing! Thursday evening of next week!"

That was it. An open house would be perfect. They were the accepted social affairs for bringing together girls and boys for an evening of fun without any of them having to have dates. Invitations went out to as many as the hostess wished and they came singly, or in groups, and stayed and mixed freely—talking, dancing, listening to records, and sipping soft drinks and eating cookies and sandwiches. Some paired off and walked home together but there was no rule about it.

It would be a fine opportunity to find out if Jenny fitted into her new group.

"Maybe," Lauralee thought hopefully, "Jenny will decide that boys aren't so bad as she used to think, and if so we can get her a date for the Homecoming dance."

Her load of guilt was magically lifted.

Then down came gloom again. Oh, dear, she hoped that Jenny would spruce up a bit in her appearance and say a few flattering things to the boys. She devoutly hoped that Jenny wouldn't be her old self and come up with something like, "Boy, were you lousy in that game today! You couldn't hang onto a ball if it had glue on it."

A girl just simply could not endear herself to boys with that kind of talk!

Lauralee's mood brightened again the minute she stepped out the front door. Who could be downhearted in a world that glowed like molten gold? She stayed gay and happy all the way to school. Tammy Taylor sat beside her on the bus and she asked Tammy to the open house.

"Sounds like fun," Tammy replied and said she would be there. How nice it was to have friends with whom to talk on the bus! Would Jenny be jealous when she found out how many new ones she had made? Then she invited Susan Adams, who sat in the seat ahead, and Lillian Hale. Lauralee didn't know Lillian very well but the new girl was friendly with Tammy and Susan. All said they would come to her party.

"I'll be there with bells on my fingers and bells on my toes," Bud laughed as he made his way to the long rear seat that he had practically leased for the school year. "Ting-a-ling-ling."

Lauralee winced at his corniness. Most times Bud was pretty sharp and then again, when one was least expecting it, he came up with a remark as idiotic as that one.

Two other freshman boys gladly accepted her invitation. One nice thing about an open house: you could invite practically *everybody*.

Things were working out fine, just as Dad always said they did, sooner or later.

Elena looked happy enough to burst, too, with some kind of good news, but she held off while Lauralee asked her to the open house.

"I will come," she smiled, "and happy, too." Then she launched her own rocket of surprise. "The Slosheks will be moving soon!"

Lauralee turned slowly and gave her friend a horrified look. "Not out of town, I hope."

Elena's head bobbed up and down, not even a tiny shadow of regret clouding her rainbow of happiness. "Yes," she said, "to a small town in the state, south."

"Oh, no!" Lauralee wailed, so loud, that several girls close by turned and looked at her curiously. But she couldn't help it. First Jenny and now Elena! It just wasn't fair that she should lose so many friends. Mother had said she would be saying hello and good-bye to folks all her life, but this was overdoing it.

Elena rushed on. "It has been, what you say, in the works for some time, this new position for my father." She emphasized the word "position." "Mr. Cramer has been trying to place him where, as he says, my father's talents will be put to better use than as a gardener." She turned to Lauralee and explained, "In the old country my father was well known for his work with plants. He was, what you call it, a botanist."

"But, but . . ." Lauralee could only sputter.

"He will work for a big seed company." Elena's eyes shone. "Improving different strains of plants and developing new ones, the work he loves."

Lauralee gulped. How could she be so selfish as not to wish the Slosheks well? Even if it did mean giving up Elena?

"I'm so happy for all of you," she said then and meant it.

Elena nodded and waved at a passing friend. "Mr. Cramer," she said warmly, "has been so kind." Lauralee managed a laugh.

"I'll say he has. Been kind to us, too, letting us use his coach house and the pony cart and all." She faced Elena then, her emotions under better control, she hoped.

Then a shadow did pass over Elena's beaming face.

"That is the only hard part," she said, her voice choking. "Leaving you and all the friends I have made here. But"—she brightened—"it won't be like losing you altogether. We will come back, sometimes, to Elm Park, and maybe sometime you can come down to see me."

"Of course, we'll see each other." Lauralee's anxiety changed to hope. "More often than we think we will." She was thinking of Jenny and how last summer it had seemed they were parting forever and now—why, next week they would see each other again. One never really lost one's friends, after all.

"When will you move?" Lauralee asked then.

"About the first of the year."

Lauralee squeezed Elena's arm. "Then we will have Homecoming and the holidays together, won't we?"

"Oh, yes!"

They parted, and a minute later Annie stopped Lauralee.

"I'm having a mixer at my house after the Homecoming dance," Annie said and it was easy to see she was happy about it. "Will you and Bud come?"

"Of course we will." Then Lauralee asked Annie to her open house and that was all settled. Sally Buskirk waved at her and she asked Sally to the open house and for a few minutes she was so busy with new friends that she forgot completely her sorrow at Elena's news. When she did remember, she realized that Elena's moving wasn't going to be the shattering experience that Jenny's going had been, and she knew why. Elena was a good friend but she wasn't her one and only!

Later that day Elena stopped her and asked if she would go shopping with her that afternoon. "For my birthday," Elena said shyly, "my father and mother gave me money. They said I should buy new dress and shoes for the Homecoming dance. You have such good taste I like you to help me pick them out."

"I'll be glad to," Lauralee replied with enthusiasm. "I love to shop!"

Lauralee started to tell her then that it wasn't just her own taste involved in the smart clothes she wore, that much of it was her mother's. But she felt so flattered she didn't.

"We'll meet out front," she said instead. "Masons' have some darling dresses on sale."

They took their time that afternoon. Elena tried on dress after dress until they both settled on a sheer wool in a soft shade of rosy beige that really did things for Elena in a nice, understated way. With its soft shawl collar and smartly flared skirt it needed no other ornament than the pin that came with it.

In the shoe department they bought black heels and a clutch bag to match.

"You'll be the belle of the ball!" laughed Lauralee, feeling pleased with their purchases.

A few minutes later she said good-bye to Elena.

"Remember we're to meet about seven thirty at the Cramer garage," she said, "to put a few finishing touches on the float."

"And the geese, no?" Elena reminded her.

"And the geese. Dad said he would drive me over with them. And Annie and Leslie and Helen will be there, too. Oh, boy, I can hardly wait until that float starts out in the big parade!"

"Let us hope it does not rain or snow that day."

"It just better not!"

Binky said he wanted to go along that evening. One of his best buddies lived next door to the Cramers and he'd drop in there while work was going on on the float. Dad was going to drop them off and then go on to some committee meeting or other.

"I'll be back around nine to pick you up," he said.

The geese were carefully placed on the back seat of the car. Dad, Lauralee, and Binky sat in front and, in no time at all, they had drawn up before the driveway leading to the Cramer garage.

"Aren't they beautiful?" Annie asked as, one by one, Lauralee lifted the geese up onto the "grass" on the bed of the truck and carefully spaced them beside the cart and the papier-mâché donkey with satin reins.

"Terrific!" the others said admiringly. Then Elena jumped up and postured as though, slim stick in hand, she was driving them.

Lauralee spied a tandem bicycle ranged along the wall of the garage beside several other such curiosities.

"Let's ride it," she giggled to Helen.

"Let's," replied Helen. The others were on the other side of the truck and didn't see them until they rode grandly out the door of the garage—and almost into Binky and his pal, Ted. Lauralee quickly caught the panic-stricken look on Elena's face when she saw them and realized that the girl didn't approve of their taking the bicycle.

"We'll just ride out to the street and then back," she said to Helen, who had seen the look, too, and nodded.

They were quickly back and set the bicycle back where it had been.

"Let me and Ted ride it!" cried Binky, who hadn't seen Elena's expression.

"Oh, no!" cried Lauralee. "Mr. Cramer wouldn't like it."

"You rode it," Binky accused.

"I know but I shouldn't have."

Elena came up then.

"We promised not to touch anything else in the garage," she said.

"Aw, I never have any fun!"

A horn tooted from the street. "There's Dad!" cried Lauralee, relieved.

Thoughts of the beautiful float occupied her mind on the ride home, and set her spirits singing. How proud all the freshmen would be when they saw their float coming down the street in the big parade!

"Some decorating committee we had!" they would say and mean it as a real compliment. She could be proud to be just a part of it.

Then she arrived home and reread Jenny's last letter.

"It will be wonderful to be together again," Jenny had written, "just we two."

Lauralee drifted into an uneasy sleep thinking about that.

16

Borrowing Trouble

"This is the big day, isn't it?"

Maxine grinned at her sister as they rushed around tidying their room one morning the next week.

"This is the day Jenny arrives!" she added as she picked up a stray book and stacked it with her others.

Lauralee did not answer for a moment. Instead she plucked a shoe from a rack in the closet, hobbled back to a chair, and sat down. She put the shoe on and then, staring down at the toe, she answered in a low, tense voice, "Yes, and you know what? I'm sort of scared."

Maxine turned and stared at her as though she had suddenly taken leave of her senses. "Scared! For goodness' sake! Of what?"

Lauralee looked blankly down at the brown flat she had matched up with a black one.

"I-I-I don't know exactly," she giggled nervously. She looked up at Maxine. "But haven't you ever looked forward to something a lot and then, when it was about to happen, gotten all skittery about it?"

Maxine sat down in a chair with a plump. "Everybody

has, I suppose," she replied softly, "about some things. But I can't understand why you should feel that way about seeing Jenny. You certainly know you enjoyed having her around—you two always seemed to have such good times together." Maxine's eyes suddenly widened. "You mean you don't want her to come? After all the mooning around you've done since she left?"

Lauralee jumped up and exchanged the black shoe for a brown one.

"Oh, no!" she cried, horrified that anyone should think such a thing. "It isn't that. It's just that—well, things won't be the same as they were before, and Jenny won't like that. I know she won't. And she's been looking forward so to coming back and seeing me." Her voice trailed off to almost a whisper.

Maxine shook her head in the manner of a person who simply cannot understand such a childish point of view. "I still can't see. . . ."

Lauralee stood up and smoothed down the pleats of her brown skirt. Then, beginning to gather her own books together, she tried to explain. "Well, she's going to expect things to be exactly the same as they were when she left, and they just won't be, that's all."

Maxine's patience was wearing thin. "Well, of course they won't be. She lives in California now and you live here and, well, you've been going your separate ways and"— she shrugged—"*some* things are bound to have changed."

Lauralee whirled on her.

"That's just it!" she cried. "Some things have changed— like me, for instance. Now I have quite a few friends and when she comes it can't be just the two of us together, like it used to be. And that is what she expects. So she will misunderstand. . . ." Her shoulders slumped in dejection at thought of her insurmountable problem.

Maxine started for the door, her arms loaded with books.

"But I thought the open house was to be the paddle that would stir her into the crowd. That's what you said, you know. It was to get her a date for the dance, and all that."

"It was, but, well, knowing Jenny like I do, it won't work! She'll be just like a fish out of water."

Maxine laughed. "Oh, come now, Lee; you're borrowing trouble."

"Lee! Max! Your breakfast is ready!" It was Dad's no-nonsense voice and it sent them scurrying down the stairs.

"I hope you're right." Lauralee sounded without hope though.

Then disgust at herself rose within her. Such mixed-up emotions! First she wanted something, then she didn't; what seemed like a good idea one minute turned into a dud the next. Honestly!

Was it selfishness on her part? She did so want to enjoy her first Homecoming weekend in high school. Jenny might easily spoil it.

Jenny, she had to admit, could be as stubborn as the proverbial mule when she wanted to be. And if she still felt the way she had about boys, she could easily turn the open house into a shambles, alienate some of the friends Lauralee had worked so hard to get, and ruin the pleasure of the dance.

Why couldn't Jenny have come some other weekend

when there were no school festivities and she had no date? Then they could have been together all the time, just the two of them.

She was absent-minded at breakfast.

"Lauralee," Mother reminded her gently, "you will be late for the bus."

Dad rattled his paper and *that* brought her out of her daze!

"Remember, dear," Mother's voice trailed her to the kitchen, "this afternoon after school we go to the airport to meet Jenny."

As if she didn't know that! But, of course, Mother expected her to be overjoyed at the prospect, and she should be. Only it seemed it just didn't work out that way.

"What's come over her?" Dad's slightly exasperated voice followed Mother's. "Moping around like a sick cat."

"Moping?" Out in the hallway Mother's voice was quite clear. "I hadn't noticed, dear."

Lauralee fled out the front door. Mother had noticed and she knew it. Why couldn't she keep her feelings to herself as Max did?

The gay greetings at the bus stop were heartwarming. She forgot Jenny momentarily. It was nice to have faces light up at sight of you, to have many friends. It came back to her more forcefully than ever that she could not go back to that *we two* business again.

Elena met her at the steps as usual. But what a different Elena this morning, her dark brows knit together in a deep frown and her usually smiling lips pressed into a thin line! Was Elena beginning to realize the implications of moving from Elm Park, the sad things like giving up friends and leaving familiar places?

Elena took her arm gravely. "Something terrible," she whispered, "it happened last night."

"What in the world . . . ?"

Elena kept her voice very low. "You remember, do you not, the tandem bicycle in Mr. Cramer's garage?"

"You mean the one Helen and I rode?"

Elena nodded. "It is gone!" she said flatly.

"But *I* didn't take it."

"I know that. But someone did, and my father says that Mr. Cramer seems to think one of us did!"

"Oh, no!" The very thought left Lauralee thunderstruck. "When was it first missed?"

"Late yesterday afternoon," Elena replied. She went on to tell how her father had opened the garage to get a few tools with which to trim back some rose bushes. He left the door open while he did it but he was gone only half an hour. When he returned the bicycle was gone. He shut the garage door and told Mr. Cramer.

Elena shuddered as she repeated her father's description of Mr. Cramer's reaction. The old man had said immediately, "Must have been those high school kids. That's what I get for letting them use my garage to build their float in. Young hoodlums, that's what young folks are nowadays."

"He didn't say *that?*"

Elena nodded mutely, and the tears springing to her eyes hinted that he had said even worse things.

"But who would want the old thing? Nobody but Helen and me so much as looked at it."

Then, suddenly Lauralee remembered something that jarred her right down to her toes. Binky had noticed it. He had wanted to ride it, too! Was her brother guilty? Her own brother! How could she think such a thing?

Still he had spent yesterday afternoon, after school, at Ted's house and Ted lived next door to the Cramers. And he could get himself into the squeakiest situations sometimes.

Fervently she hoped that the news of the missing bicycle spread no further until the whole thing was cleared up, without Binky being involved if possible.

The rumor started slowly at first and, as rumors will, gathered momentum until, before the day was many hours older, it was all over the school. *A freshman had stolen a bicycle from the Cramer garage!*

Mr. Cramer, it seemed, had called the principal of Willowlake that morning to report the missing bicycle and tell his views of the matter. Mr. Callison had calmly told him he would look into the situation.

And he did by discreetly calling in Annie and Leslie and asking them a couple of questions without accusing anybody of anything. As Leslie left the office one of his friends had asked him why he had been called on the carpet, and Leslie had indignantly denied any such thing, and had told the truth. It was like touching a match to a pile of dry leaves.

The finger of suspicion had been pointed, and those at whom it was pointed were furious about it.

The day seemed endless to Lauralee. She fairly leaped from the bus, she was so anxious to get home and hear from Binky's own lips that he had had nothing to do with that tandem bicycle and that they could jolly well look elsewhere for their old bicycle thief.

Something led her to the garage. In she went and her eyes scanned the shadowy interior. She almost fainted—for there, in the rear, half-hidden by the mower, a big basket, Dad's yard cart, and rakes and hoes, stood the very thing she dreaded most to see—the tandem bicycle! There could be only one bright yellow one with shining black trim, and that had been the one in the Cramer garage!

"Oh, no!" she moaned and fled into the house.

Mother met her in the hallway.

"I've been waiting for you, dear," Mrs. Larkin smiled, pulling on her gloves. "We have just time to get to the airport to meet Jenny and her father and grandmother."

Gently she hurried a dazed Lauralee out the front door again.

Jenny! It was the first time Lauralee had thought of Jenny since she had got off the bus in front of school that morning. How could Mother so nonchalantly go out to the airport to meet *anybody* at a time like this?

Briskly her mother walked to the garage of the house next door. Mrs. Jason, an old lady of about eighty years, lived there all alone, and the Larkins rented her garage and kept Mrs. Larkin's small car there.

Numbly Lauralee followed her mother and got into the car. Only then did she appreciate the reason for Mother's nonchalance. She didn't know a thing about a certain tandem bicycle!

Should she tell her mother? Certainly she would have to know, sooner or later.

The motor of the small car purred as they backed out into

the street, and soon they were on their way toward Park Ridge and O'Hare field.

When they were within sight of the huge field she blurted out her story. Mother's sweet expression turned so shocked and pained that Lauralee would have done anything to spare her.

"Are you sure of what you say, Lee?" Mrs. Larkin asked softly.

Lauralee sniffed. "I only wish I weren't," she moaned.

Mother turned into the stream of traffic going into the field.

"Well, let's take things one at a time. We'll meet the Moores just as we had planned. Not a word of this to them, mind you, not until we have talked to Binky."

"Don't worry." Lauralee slid down into her seat and wished with all her heart she was somewhere else, *anywhere*. "I'm not anxious to spread it around."

Gloom clouded the faces of both as the car inched its way through the swarming parking section while planes roared overhead. Mother found an open space and squeezed into it. They stepped out and stood near a little shed with a sign over it that said SHUTTLE-BUS STOP. Soon a tiny bus came by and took them to the farther-away-than-it-looked terminal.

"I should look happy and gay," Lauralee thought miserably as they stepped from the bus onto an escalator that took them up into the terminal. "But I don't."

Mother, usually so warmly cheerful, wasn't feeling any better, Lauralee knew. Mrs. Larkin loved meeting and greeting people. Now her mind was on other things as she led the way through the milling throng—passengers buying tickets and checking baggage, porters hurrying about helping bewildered newcomers, people waiting for arrivals or saying good-bye to others about to depart.

Everything was so confusing. Feeling like a sleepwalker, Lauralee followed the trim figure of her mother down the long passageway to the gates where the plane from California would come in.

"Gate seven the man at the desk said," Mother told her breathlessly. She was half-running now as the jet was due in two minutes.

They reached gate seven just in time to see the plane taxi in and the ground crew roll out the ramp and place it against the side of the metal monster.

A young lady in the natty blue suit of a hostess stepped out first. Then came the passengers. For one brief instant Lauralee forgot everything else and craned her neck, eagerly searching for her friend.

"There is Grandma Moore," she said as a short, stout lady came down the steps followed by a tall, balding man. "And Mr. Moore."

But where was Jenny? A smartly clad young lady clicked on high heels in front of Mr. Moore and his mother, and two young men were behind them, and then came an older woman.

"There's Jenny," said Mother, a rising note of excitement creeping into her voice, in spite of her trouble.

"Where?"

"Why, right ahead of them, the one with the lovely hairdo. See, she's waving."

Lauralee stared. Could that chic girl in the trimly fitting suit be Jenny?

Now they were through the gate. It was Jenny all right; she could not mistake the round, rosy face or the startlingly blue eyes around which the skin crinkled so engagingly when she laughed.

Suddenly all the old love she had ever felt for her friend welled up within Lauralee.

"Jenny!" she shrieked joyously and made a mad dash for her. She hugged her friend to her, then held her off at arm's length. "My, how nice you look!"

"And *you!* Terrific!" They hugged again and Jenny whispered in her ear, "Just think—the two of us together again!" And her friend squeezed her arm in the old familiar way, as though loath ever to let her go. Then Jenny whispered fiercely, "We'll have fun these next few days!" Her voice rose. "Fun, fun, FUN!"

Lauralee's heart sank like a stone at Jenny's squeal. Fun, did she say? How could she have fun when tomorrow everybody in the whole world would know about Binky and that bicycle? But Jenny didn't know about it now, and she couldn't tell her.

"Oh, boy, we sure will," was her lifeless answer. Jenny looked at her wonderingly. *Well, if the prospect leaves you that cold,* her look seemed to say.

Lauralee tried to ignore the look. Jenny wouldn't want her as a friend anyway come tomorrow. So what was the use in trying to erase Jenny's mistaken impression?

Mr. Moore's booming voice cut in then, "It was good of you to meet us! Now, I'll see you ladies to your car and then

I'll take a limousine to my hotel in the Loop." He turned to Mrs. Larkin. "That's where the convention I'm attending is being held and, as I shall be busy there day and night, I think it will be best for me to stay there until Sunday morning. Then I'll come out to Elm Park and pick up Jenny and we'll fly back to the coast that afternoon."

It had all been prearranged and he had soon stowed the luggage belonging to his daughter and mother into the Larkin car and was on his way back to the terminal and the limousine.

Grandma Moore settled herself in the front seat beside Mrs. Larkin, and Jenny and Lauralee, rather stiff toward each other now, climbed in the back seat.

Lauralee's unenthusiastic response to her wholehearted "have-fun" suggestion had apparently stabbed deeply into Jenny's feelings. Now her attitude was a cold, *Well, it's your move next*. Lauralee knew it, but for the life of her she could not make the move. She just sat like a bump on a log, in gloomy silence.

When the last of the luggage had been taken into Grandma Moore's home, Lauralee turned to Jenny and said listlessly, "I'll be by in the morning for you to go to school."

Jenny gave her a long, cool look. "Well, if it isn't too much *trouble*," she said and walked away.

Lauralee watched her go, sorrow stiffening her lips. If Jenny only knew!

Borrowing trouble? Would Maxine say that now?

17

Time Will Tell

Binky squirmed.

"But we weren't going to *keep* it!" he cried, his eyes wide with astonishment that anyone should think such a thing. "We were just going to ride on it and have a little fun and then—"

Dad was patient as always, though stern. "Better start at the beginning," he directed.

Binky hunched miserably.

"Well, Ted and I were horsin' around in the Taylors' yard and our ball went through the Cramers' hedge. Well, we went after it and we saw the garage door open and Mr. Sloshek leaving." He gulped. "Then I saw the old bike." He looked up at Lauralee. "The one you and Helen were riding the other evening."

Lauralee's mouth flew open. It was the first time she had thought of it that way, that she had really been the first to take the bicycle out of the garage! *She* had been responsible in part!

"But I put it back right away," she protested.

"Go on," Dad said to Binky.

"Well, I thought it would be fun to ride it, too, and I talked Ted into it." Swinging his legs aimlessly, Binky went on almost in a whisper. "It was mostly my fault and I don't want to get Ted into trouble. Well, we got the bike out and decided to ride it around the block, but we were going to put it right back, honest."

His eyes roved over his listeners—Lauralee, Maxine, Mother and Dad, as though seeking approval of his good intentions. Meeting with reproving stares, he turned his gaze down to the toes of his shoes and stammered on, "Well, we rode it longer than we thought we would and when we got back the garage door was closed and locked." He squirmed again. "We *couldn't* put it back!" His eyes were appealing. "So we thought we'd put it in the Taylor garage until we got a chance to put it where it belonged. Then we found that Mr. Taylor was cleaning out their garage and we couldn't put it there." He looked straight at his father. "He'd ask questions, you know."

"Very likely," Dad said drily.

"We didn't know where else to put it so we brought it over here."

Mr. Larkin's stern gaze softened. "Didn't you think of looking for Mr. Sloshek and telling him what you had done and taking the consequences right then and there?"

Binky pursed his lips. "Yes, we thought of it, but. . . ."

"But you didn't act upon it, right? So, as is usually the case when you put things off, you made things much worse." Mr. Larkin straightened up. "Now it is all over the school that some freshman stole that bicycle—one of the decoration committee being the most likely suspect."

"I'm sorry about that," Binky muttered.

"I didn't see it in the garage this morning or—well, we must think of some way of getting all those freshmen off the hook. What would you suggest, Binky?"

Binky stared long and hard at a frayed place on the knee of his corduroy trousers. Then he gulped and whispered hoarsely, "I can confess." And he explained what he thought he ought to do.

His father slapped him on the shoulder, a pleased look on his face. "Good boy! I'll call Mr. Callison and ask his opinion of the matter."

He went straight to the telephone in the hallway and dialed the number of the principal of Willowlake Community High School. He told of Binky's involvement in the matter of the missing bicycle, his regret of it, and Binky's plan to make up for the trouble he had caused.

Mr. Callison agreed to call the entire freshman class into the school auditorium the first thing next day so Binky could tell all of them how he and a friend, unnamed, had taken the bicycle as a prank. He would apologize and say how sorry he was that they had suffered because of his thoughtless action.

He and his father would personally return the bicycle to Mr. Cramer with more apologies.

"And that," said father, "should do the trick. And also teach you a lesson, young man."

"Yes, sir," Binky replied meekly.

Lauralee sat numbly and stared out the window while all this was going on. Do the trick, Dad had said. It certainly would! It would ruin her at school forever and ever! How she would suffer! The very thought of sitting through such an assembly tomorrow sent her into agonies of distress.

Next morning Lauralee awakened with no desire to go to school—with Jenny or otherwise. But she had to, and so she went through the motions of getting ready. The morning meal was eaten in silence. Dad wasn't going in to the office until noon because of the things he and Binky had to do together.

"Bye, everybody," Lauralee said as she left to go over to Grandma Moore's house for her friend. Only a murmur came back as a reply.

Jenny's grandparents lived in a house just two buildings away from the one formerly belonging to her parents. Lauralee approached it with dread. How could she sit through that assembly this morning, with Jenny beside her, and listen to Binky pour out his tale of guilt?

Was it all Binky's guilt? Didn't you take the bicycle out first? The voice of her conscience had been dim at first but it was growing louder with each passing minute. Impatiently she tried to shut it from her consciousness. *Don't be silly,* she told herself grimly. *He should have known better than to do what he did. He should have thought of all the trouble he might cause others, especially me.*

A tide of resentment against Binky washed over her. The dope! After all the effort she had made to acquire new friends, she was losing them because of him!

"Jenny's luckier'n I am," she thought resentfully. "She doesn't have any old brother."

Grandma Moore opened the door. "Why, good morning, Lauralee," she said cheerfully. "Do come in. Jenny will be down in a minute." She turned then to the stairs in the hallway. "Jenny dear, Lauralee's here."

"Be down in a minute," came back the indifferent reply.

Lauralee sat down to wait. It was beginning already, this coolness toward her. *But she doesn't know about Binky yet!* Binky was to blame for everything. If it hadn't been for him things would have gone differently on the way from the airport yesterday afternoon.

Jenny came slowly down the stairs then, in the manner of an actress entering a ballroom. She was dressed like a fashion model and didn't look at all like the old Jenny, who would have tumbled down the stairs, buttoning as she came.

"Hi, Lauralee." Jenny's voice was so coolly impersonal that Lauralee winced. But then, she might as well get accustomed to such treatment from her once-upon-a-time friends. After this morning, they would all treat her the same way. "Nice of you to come by for me."

There was a trace of sarcasm in the last remark that Lauralee preferred to ignore, knowing well the reason for it. Binky! The whole sorry mess was his fault.

On the way to the bus stop, Jenny's manner toward her was as distant as though they had met for the first time. They spoke to each other only about generalities.

But the minute Jenny saw Bud her colors changed like those of a chameleon. Approaching him as if he were her long lost brother, she cried, "Why, Bud Newton, how glad I am to see you!"

Jenny had changed, all right. She would fit into the crowd. If there *was* a crowd any more.

Jenny slipped her hand possessively through the crook of his arm and Bud, rising to the occasion, chatted and talked with her in the same manner he had once used toward Eloise Fisher.

"Looks like California has treated you pretty well!" Lauralee did not miss the remark or the appreciative looks he gave the new Jenny.

"Oh, it has, but I love Elm Park and miss all my friends here."

All her friends! And she gave no look at Lauralee.

In a way Lauralee was glad it had worked out this way. She would have been poor company, glum as she was on the ride to school. Nobly she decided that she wouldn't want Jenny's visit spoiled by her troubles.

She needn't have worried. Bud and Jenny sat together on the back seat of the bus and laughed and chatted and had a great time. Soon they were mobbed by three obviously admiring boys and Tammy and Eileen and others, all asking about California, and how Jenny liked it.

"They don't even know I'm alive," Lauralee thought and slid down further into her own gloom.

It was the same after they had stepped off the bus. This new, slick chick was surrounded by boys, Robert Lee soon joining the cheering section. It was easy to see that Jenny was really attracted to *him*.

Then came a short homeroom period and Mr. Callison's voice over the public address system announcing the assembly of the freshman class. The room buzzed with speculation as to why a special assembly had been called. Numbly Lauralee went with the others.

"Will he be at the open house tonight?" Jenny asked suddenly.

"Who?"

"Why, that nice southern boy, Stonewall something or other."

"Oh, you mean Robert Lee? Well, I *asked* him."

Lauralee's mouth felt as dry as cotton. After this assembly would anybody show up at her party tonight?

"I don't care whether anybody does or not!" she told herself fiercely as she sat down beside Jenny.

Jenny looked at her queerly. "What *is* the matter with you?" she whispered.

Lauralee's mouth opened but no words came out, for at that moment Mr. Callison strode onto the stage. He looked grave this morning.

"I have called this assembly for a very special reason," he said. "As you remember, a rumor went the rounds yesterday that a certain tandem bicycle had been reported missing by its owner."

During his pause Lauralee shut her eyes tight and clenched her fists. Before her danced a picture of Helen and herself riding that bike out of the garage. Had she, who had talked Helen into riding it with her, been partly to blame for this whole thing? She had had no more business taking it out of the garage than Binky had. And Binky might not have seen it if she had left it where it was. She opened her eyes again, and saw Binky just off stage behind the curtain. How lonely and pathetic he looked! Her heart went out to him.

Mr. Callison went on. "As rumors will, this one stirred

up misunderstandings. In order to clear them up a young man has come to tell you all about what happened."

Should Binky face it alone?

Lauralee couldn't stand it another minute. She got up from her seat, leaving a surprised Jenny, and walked down the aisle and around the front of the stage and up the steps at one side of it. She went through the door to the space just off stage.

Without saying a word she put one arm round Binky's shoulders and squeezed. Binky looked up, surprised and pleased.

"Thanks, Lee," he said and then walked stiffly out on stage.

His voice was loud and clear when he told what he had done. He said a friend had been with him but, as it had been entirely his fault, he wouldn't mention the friend's name.

"We didn't mean any harm, honest," Binky said in closing. "And I'm as sorry as I can be for what happened."

Binky walked back toward her. How proud she was of him! She didn't care what the others thought.

Then she did something she hadn't really expected to do. She went onto the stage, too!

"May I add something to what my brother said, Mr. Callison?" she asked in a voice clear enough to be heard in the back of the big room.

"Why, certainly, Lauralee," replied the principal.

Lauralee turned to face her classmates. "It wasn't really all my brother's fault," she began. And she went on to tell how *she* had first thought of taking the bicycle out of the garage and had talked a friend of hers, unnamed, into riding the bicycle with her.

"And I'm sorry I did that, too," she said.

Amid the laughter of her classmates she walked off stage and the assembly was over. Lauralee didn't regret the step she had taken. It wasn't right that Binky should assume blame that was partly hers. And whether the audience had been laughing with her or at her wasn't important at all. If her friends didn't want to be her friends any more—well, that was their privilege.

Jenny met her first as she walked down the stage steps again.

"Was *that* the reason you've been so distant since I got here?" she demanded.

Lauralee nodded, tears welling up in spite of her best efforts to keep her emotions under control.

"Well, why didn't you tell me?" Jenny was indignant. Then she grabbed Lauralee's arm and squeezed it. "No wonder you couldn't say much. I would have been scared speechless, too, if I thought I had to go through something like that."

"Your little brother, he was very brave," Elena smiled over Jenny's shoulder. "And you, too."

Annie stopped her and said, "I'm glad *that's* over."

Bud grinned and chuckled. "Didn't know old Bink had it in him."

All of which, Lauralee believed, could be taken with a grain of salt. Would they, as well as others who greeted her in the hall just as though nothing really bad had happened, remain her friends? Or would they gradually drift away? Time would tell.

18

Day of Triumph

Would anyone come? Lauralee's face puckered anxiously into the mirror above the dressing table Elena had helped her decorate. It was almost time for her open house to start. Dressed in her best red wool, she was nervously awaiting her guests.

Jenny would come, she could be certain of that. Dear Jenny.

"See you tonight," her friend had said as she left the school building just before noon. Grandma Moore had been waiting outside to take her to a luncheon engagement.

Jenny had changed all right, but only on the outside. Underneath she was the same, loving and loyal.

Elena would be here, too, and so would Annie. Bud would come and Jim Talbot. But would the others show up? Or had all the friendships but these excepted few been wiped out after what had happened that morning?

Binky! It had all been his fault! Again her resentment rose against her small brother. Then came common sense to override it. He wasn't any more to blame, really, than she. But what a shock that morning assembly had been! She remembered little of what had happened the rest of the day except that during the last period they had voted for freshman Homecoming king and queen. She had put down the names of Robert Lee Morton and Elena, and then wondered why she hadn't chosen Bud.

Homecoming and its attendant festivities meant little to her right now.

She and Mother had been busy all afternoon getting ready for the party that night. Platefuls of finger sandwiches were stored in the refrigerator. Plenty of soda was on hand, as well as popcorn, pretzels, and cheese tidbits. Records were stacked beside the player, and paper and pencils were ready for several games Maxine had suggested. Until this minute Lauralee had been too busy to think about the fact that many of her guests might not come.

But now she was giving it a great deal of thought.

Jenny, gay and bubbly, was the first to arrive. She almost made Lauralee feel gay, too, as they sat in the living room and chatted and waited for the others.

The doorbell rang again and on the porch stood Elena and Annie and Richard. Lauralee's spirits began a slow rise.

The bell rang constantly after that and, a half hour later, she was ecstatically happy. Everyone she had asked had come!

What fun they had! Her friends loved Jenny, particularly the boys, judging from the way they hovered about her all evening.

"Did you think she'd have trouble mixing with the crowd?" Bud asked Lauralee, his eyes gleaming with mischief and suppressed laughter.

Lauralee gave him an arch look. "And did you think she'd have trouble getting a date for the dance?"

They both laughed at that, for only a few minutes before, Jenny had followed Lauralee to the kitchen and confided, "You know that nice southern boy—what's his name. . . ?"

"Robert Lee," Lauralee chuckled.

"Well, whatever—anyway, he has asked me to go to the Homecoming dance with him!" She did a little dance of her own about the kitchen, daintily tapping with the point of a manicured forefinger each appliance or utensil she passed. "You know what? I accepted his kind invitation."

"You mean *you all* are going with him?"

"I all am!"

And they both dissolved into mild hysterics.

Then something struck Lauralee. "But who is taking Eloise?" she whispered to Bud a few minutes later.

"Oh, a senior!" he said.

"Might have known!"

Of course she might have known that Eloise would not be caught short; the redhead would always be a step or so ahead of the other freshman girls. But there was one like that in every class. What did it matter anyway?

Then, before she knew it, she was bidding her guests good-bye. Jenny was the last to leave, and they hugged each other fondly.

"What a wonderful evening, Lee," Jenny said as they stood for a moment in the hallway, just talking. "It was so much fun meeting all your friends. You know what? Now I almost feel they're my friends, too."

Lauralee turned glowing eyes upon her. "Almost?" she

echoed. "Why, they *are* your friends!" She breathed deeply and sighed. "I know I'll never be so happy again in my whole life as I am tonight."

Next morning though she changed her mind.

Over the public address system were announced the names of the Homecoming kings and queens. Beginning with the senior class and progressing downward . . . junior, sophomore . . . Lauralee and the others in her homeroom became noticeably more interested.

"Freshman king," the voice intoned, "Robert Lee Morton."

"Yay," cried the class and, while he grinned modestly, one could see he was immensely pleased.

"Freshman queen, Lauralee Larkin!"

Lauralee's eyes popped and her chin dropped. She sat at her desk stunned.

"Congratulations!"

"Aren't you the lucky one?"

"Couldn't have happened to a nicer gal!"

Was it all a dream? But no, the best wishes of her classmates and the faces that smiled at her—they were real. She had been so wrong the evening before. *This* was the happiest moment she would ever experience!

The rest of that day she spent in a rosy glow. The realization of the wonderful thing that had happened to her slowly crystallized in her mind. She and Robert Lee . . . chosen monarchs for a day . . . chosen by their *friends*. How many of them she must have to make this wonderful thing happen to her!

Mental pictures of their triumphant ride down the main

streets of Elm Park came and went, each one more dazzling than the one before.

As she stepped from the bus that afternoon Jenny met her with a warm hug. "To think I can rub elbows with royalty," she giggled. "Don't you think you should at least curtsy?" Lauralee asked with mock hauteur. And Jenny did.

Binky was waiting on the front steps, a big grin stretching from ear to ear. As Lauralee and Jenny turned into the walk leading to their house, he jumped up and held one hand high.

"Your royal highness!" he cried. "There is a speck of dust on the sidewalk!" And he threw down an old ragged sweater and waved her on. She walked with mincing steps over it, almost stumbling in its folds, at which her courtier and lady-in-waiting laughed aloud.

Lauralee was glad Binky could share her triumph. He *had* looked so pathetic and alone on that stage yesterday morning. Still, the admiration her classmates had expressed for his courage in facing them might have had something to do with her election. Certainly she must have gained, rather than lost, friends that day.

Mother had already started to make her royal robe.

"It'll be cold the day of the parade," she smiled fondly. "You must be bundled up and still look queenly."

A pair of velveteen draperies, dug out of a chest full of things that Mother always felt would come in handy someday, provided the material. From it she had begun to fashion a long cape with a stand-up ruffled collar.

"Just the right color, too." Jenny admired it as Lauralee tried on the basted garment and pranced before a mirror.

"A beautiful plum shade."

"Mom thinks of everything!" Lauralee cried and kissed her mother's cheek in appreciation.

"Where do you get your crown?" Binky asked, adding hopefully, "I could make you a swell one."

Lauralee gave him a fond smile. "The art class at school is making the crowns," she said. "You know, Annie and her crowd. I hear everybody is bringing old junk jewelry and they're using the 'gems' for decoration."

If she knew Annie and her friends, they would turn out some stunning crowns and scepters. Annie, especially, was fast becoming appreciated and admired for her imagination and the lovely things she created with her clever hands. Her willingness to use her talents and abilities for the benefit of others was becoming well known, too. Annie's popularity was growing by leaps and bounds.

Jenny seemed to revel in Lauralee's success at being elected Homecoming queen. "You must really be popular and have a lot of friends," she said admiringly and without a trace of the jealousy she would have shown a year ago.

After Jenny had left, and she and Mother were preparing dinner, Lauralee spoke of it. "Things *seem* the same between me and Jenny," she said as she vigorously brushed the big potatoes for baking. "Yet they're different, too."

Mother smiled at her. "You're growing up, that's all," she said softly. "You are both changing; your worlds are becoming larger. Change, after all, is the normal state of things." While Lauralee wrapped the potatoes in foil she turned on the oven. "Things are never exactly the same today as they were yesterday."

Dad beamed proudly at the news.

"That's my girl!" he cried. He turned to his wife. "Do we have film enough in that movie camera for the parade?"

"I bought some today," was Mother's reply.

Lauralee floated on a cloud of pure bliss until Saturday morning; then her happiness became even more overwhelming.

The floats, a bewildering number of them, gathered early that morning in the parking lot behind the high school and overflowed into the driveway that circled about the big main building.

Every organized group or club at school, it seemed, had entered a float, and its members had spent long and dedicated hours working on it. Some were huge, elaborate creations and some were small and simple. Those using the "Hands Across the Sea" theme had kept to the countries of the two exchange students, Japan and Ireland.

"There are dragons and leprechauns all over the place!" Lauralee laughed as Dad helped her up onto the freshman float.

"And pagodas and shamrocks," he added as he gave her a fond wave and went back to the crowd of watchers.

"Ours is different," cried Robert Lee as he sat down beside her in the cart. He picked up the reins of the donkey and playfully slapped the papier-mâché animal with it. Then he added *"Vive la différence!"*

Lauralee giggled. "You're just showing off your freshman French," she said. "Besides this is a sort of Moravian-Austrian design."

"Well, whatever it is, I like it." The southern boy tilted his crown to a more jaunty angle and gave the watchers a regally languid wave of the hand. That brought a howl and a wad of paper sailing in his direction.

"Off with his head!" he shouted and pointed at the offender.

The air was charged with gaiety. Everyone was in high spirits. Even the weather contributed to the festive feeling. The sun was shining bright and clear and the air was just briskly cool enough to make moving about a pleasure.

Each class had a float. The senior creation was a towering pagoda with the senior king and queen standing before it. It was done in black, vermilion, and gold and swayed so on the truck that it took two stout athletes, dressed as Japanese wrestlers, to keep it from toppling.

"Wait until we go over the North Western tracks!" laughed one.

"Especially if a stiff breeze springs up!" replied the other.

There was much laughter and shouts and good-natured raillery as the floats were placed in line. Miss Harrison, head of the art department, went up and down the line suggesting changes for color effect.

The freshman float was put in the middle. Mr. Sloshek, in Alpine pants, colorfully embroidered vest, and peaked cap with a tall feather stuck in the band, climbed into the flower-bedecked cab of the truck and wheeled it into line.

Elena dashed through the crowd then and clambered up onto the truck. She took her position, sparklingly lovely, behind her "geese."

Robert Lee turned and grinned back at her. "Honey,

Ah'm shuah glad y'all came to take care of those geese,"
he said. "They were flying around all ovah the place!"

"They will fly no more," Elena grinned back.

A police car, its red light flashing, passed them then,
on its way to the head of the parade.

"We're about to start!" Lauralee's eyes shone with excitement as she turned to Robert Lee. "Hadn't we better begin
being sort of dignified and royal looking?"

" 'Spect so," he agreed and they sat stiff and straight
as ramrods for a couple of minutes. The *oompah* of the band
floated back to them then and the line started moving slowly. Out of the school grounds it wound and on down through
the main streets of Elm Park.

The crowds were thickest in the business section. People
were lined up two and three deep along the sidewalks in
front of stores. They clapped and shouted as the police
car appeared. Then they ooohed and ahhhed as each float
passed by.

Behind the police car came a small compact convertible,
draped in black, gold, and vermilion. Sitting on its let-
down top was Jennie Matsuko, dressed in a kimono and
looking like a beautiful Japanese doll. Behind her came
another compact convertible draped in green and bearing
a smiling Mary Kelly.

The senior float got over the tracks all right, but there
were a few anxious seconds as the pagoda tilted at a danger-
ous angle. It righted itself, however, and went on, to the
delight of the crowd.

The freshman float was received with applause and
praise all along the route—doubly meaningful to Lauralee

because she had shared in the hard work of making it beautiful. Robert Lee clowned constantly, mockingly beating the donkey with his cardboard scepter. His crown kept falling off and Elena good-humoredly picked it up and handed it back.

"Between your crown and my geese," she scolded, "a busy time I am having." She waved her stick at Annie David, watching on the sidelines, tears of pride mistily showing behind her glasses. Beside Annie were Eloise and Eileen and Marion Avery, their faces glowing with pride, too.

"Behave yourselves up there!" Eloise called with a toss of her bright red hair. "We want a prize on that float, you know."

If there was any rancor on Eloise's part at not being queen this year, she did not let it show. She had wanted to be queen and had made it plain. Had she decided that, not having been elected, she'd not be a poor sport about it? Did even Eloise have to adjust sometimes?

Then Lauralee spied Jenny on a corner, sitting on the curb. Grandma Moore stood right behind her. Jenny waved at her and Robert Lee and they waved back, and at that minute Grandma raised her camera and took a picture.

And there was Dad, standing up tall so as to see over the shoulders of people in front of him. He aimed his small movie camera right at her. She could hear him saying to those around him, "That's my daughter, there, the queen on the freshman float."

He would soon be showing those pictures to anyone willing to watch.

Mother was beside him, a yellow scarf over her head

and a giant golden mum pinned to the collar of her car coat. She waved a gloved hand as the float went by. Bud, standing with several members of the football squad, beamed at her.

Toward the end of the route, out of sheer exuberance, she and Robert Lee slid off the seat of the cart and picked a few of the paper flowers from the back of the cab and threw them to the thinning crowd.

What a day of triumph it had been! And there was more to come!

The first prize went to the freshman float! On the basis of originality, beauty, and adherence to theme, it was voted top honors by the panel of judges.

"Some float we had!" Lauralee cried happily as she and Annie and Elena and the rest of the decorating committee bubbled over the decision. She said nothing about the origin of the remark.

That afternoon she and Robert Lee and Elena were the cynosure of all eyes as, during halftime of the big game, the winning float was drawn across the field to the music of the band.

The excitement carried over into the evening when Bud arrived to take her to the dance. How nice he looked in a new tweed sport jacket and brown flannel slacks!

Mrs. Newton stopped by for Robert Lee and Jenny and took the four of them to the school. Later Lauralee's happiness exploded like a rocket as the orchestra leader announced, one by one, the class queens and their escorts, and she and Bud walked in the spotlight to the center of the dance floor. Then he announced the kings and their partners, and Robert Lee and Jenny were standing beside them. She and Jenny squeezed each other's hands. Then the royal couples led the grand march around the floor.

Yes, things had changed since they had left junior high school but neither Lauralee nor Jenny would have wanted it otherwise!

"I'll remember this day as long as I live," Lauralee said to Bud as they parted that night at her front door.

"Me, too," he nodded and grinned sleepily. "It was great."

Before he turned to leave he squeezed her hand affectionately and added, "But there'll be others just as good—maybe even better."

"I don't doubt that," was her reply.

She could even smile happily the next afternoon when she bade Jenny good-bye at the airport.

"I had a tremendous time," Jenny smiled as they embraced. "Mostly thanks to you."

Lauralee hugged her friend hard. Strange, she had many friends now but she loved Jenny none the less.

"There'll be others just as good," she whispered, "maybe even better."

"You bet there will," and Jenny was through the gate and gone.

Tears welled up then in Lauralee's eyes, but she quickly brushed them aside. What was there to cry for? Ahead lay many bright and shining tomorrows with her own charmed circle that was growing bigger every day.